D1524443

C'Yani & Meek 2

A Dangerous Hood Love

Tina J

Copyright 2018

More Books by Tina J

A Thin Line Between Me & My Thug 1-2
I Got Luv for My Shawty 1-2
Kharis and Caleb: A Different kind of Love 1-2
Loving You is a Battle 1-3
Violet and the Connect 1-3
You Complete Me
Love Will Lead You Back
This Thing Called Love
Are We in This Together 1-3
Shawty Down to Ride For a Boss 1-3
When a Boss Falls in Love 1-3
Let Me Be The One 1-2
We Got That Forever Love
Ain't No Savage Like The One I got 1-2
A Queen & Hustla 1-3 (collab)
Thirsty for a Bad Boy 1-2
Hasaan and Serena: An Unforgettable Love 1-2
We Both End Up With Scars
Caught up Luvin a beast 1-3
A Street King & his Shawty 1-2
I Fell for the Wrong Bad Boy 1-2 (collab)
Addicted to Loving a Boss 1-3
All Eyes on the Crown 1-3
I Need that Gangsta Love 1-2 (collab)
Still Luvin' a Beast 1-2
Creepin' With The Plug 1-2
I Wanna Love You 1-2
Her Man, His Savage 1-2
When She's Bad, I'm Badder 1-3
Marco & Rakia 1-3
Feenin' for a Real One 1-3
A Kingpin's Dynasty 1-3
What Kind Of Love Is This?
Frankie & Lexi 1-3
A Dope Boy's Seduction 1-3
My Brother's Keeper 1-3
C'Yani & Meek 1-3

Previously…

"She's gonna be mad." Shak joked about C'Yani being upset. He stopped by to see me and as usual, one thing led to another with us. Ever since we began sleeping together, it's like we couldn't keep our hands off.

"I know but something had to be wrong for her to be banging the way she was." He handed me my shirt.

"Let's go see." He opened the door and Jasmine was standing there.

"What the fuck you standing outside the door for?"

"Shak." I touched his arm and he pushed past her with an attitude.

"Let's go see what your sister wanted." He pulled me away and remained quiet the rest of the way.

"Please don't tell me you slept with her." He stopped before we got to C'Yani's door and moved the hair out my face.

"I would never sleep with someone who…" He cut himself off.

5

"I've never slept with her and I told you from the very beginning she's sneaky. Something ain't right with her Teri."

"Her attitude sucks but she good peoples." He ignored me and opened the door to my sister's office. If my sister was white, her face would be beet red. That's how angry she looked.

"How dare you invite that woman to work here without notifying me first?" Shak stared at me.

"This is supposed to be our building. I didn't know each person I hired had to go through you." She came over to me.

"Don't talk that nonsense to me Teri. This is a building I purchased and I'd never question anything you do and you know it. However; you are fully aware she and I don't care for one another and now she's going to run a business outta here? I will not accept it. She has to go."

"Hold the fuck up T. I know damn well she ain't talking about the bitch downstairs."

"Why does everyone hate her, and the entire floor is mine so if I want her to open up her business then I can. She

6

doesn't have to come up here, nor do you have to walk on that floor."

"So, if I want to see my sister I have to wait until we get home or if you come here?"

"If that's what you wanna do."

"T, you dead ass fucking wrong."

"I never thought my sister would pick a woman over me but you know what." She went to pick her things up.

"You do what you want because that floor is yours right?"

"Yup." I said it with my arms folded.

"Make sure you or your employee don't step one foot on this got damn floor and the grand opening will be for my business only."

"Really?"

"Really and I'm moving out."

"Moving out?" I saw Shak shaking his head.

"Yea, that's your house and I've never said a word about her coming by because it's yours. Here this is a building

I brought and you don't care how I feel about a woman not liking me work here."

"C'Yani you're not going to like everyone you work with. Is this how you'll react?"

"No because I wouldn't hire anyone who didn't care for me or my sister. It's a nightmare waiting to happen, which is exactly what this is. But don't worry, as long as you have your friend here."

"FINE! Move out then."

"Already in the process. Now get the hell out of my office. I need to pack." Shak looked at her and smirked. I guess he got a kick outta how she spoke.

"Good riddance." We walked out, she locked her door and stormed off. Shak wasn't too far behind.

"Shakim! Where are you going?" He turned around with an evil face.

"You're helping out a bitch who can't stand your sister."

"What is the problem?"

"Why didn't you speak to C'Yani about it?" I didn't answer because there was no reason on why I didn't.

"Yes, she gave you free range to do whatever but it's no way in hell you should've agreed to hiring her. What if she did some shit like that to you? Huh? Not only that, she couldn't wait to rub it in her face." I couldn't say a word because everything he was saying is true.

"That bitch is up to something and whether you sit in denial or not, it's going to somehow hurt your sister in the long run but all you seem to worry about is being a boss."

"Excuse me."

"C'Yani purchased this building for you and her. The only reason your name isn't on the paperwork is because you weren't there when she signed it. But you're so fucking hell bent on pleasing Jasmine, that you shitted all over C. You that desperate to be in charge?"

"I can buy my own building Shakim. My sister isn't the only one with money."

"You're not listening." He stood in my face.

"Who the fuck cares about the money? She did this for y'all." He started to walk away and turned around.

"In my eyes you have no loyalty and I can't be with a bitch like that."

"I'm a bitch now?"

"Yup because only dumb bitches do shit like you. We all know Jasmine can't stand your sister for some reason and we haven't even known you that long. Yet, you sit around and let her disrespect C on a regular and brush it off like it's her being funny."

"She doesn't have any real problems with my sister." He shook his head.

"The bitch don't like C'Yani for whatever reason and now you're forcing your sister to be uncomfortable in her place of work. What type of shit you on?"

"Shakim, don't leave." He chuckled and stared at Jasmine standing at the door. Where did she come from?

"You need to figure out your life because as long as she's in it, you're about to lose a lot more people than me and your sister. Tha fuck your stupid ass looking at?" He mushed her so hard she fell back and I heard her hit the ground.

"Shakim."

"I wish you would say something." I kept my mouth closed and followed him down the steps and out the door.

"Shak wait!"

"Wait for what Teri?"

"I don't want you to leave."

"Too bad. I suggest you make amends with your sister because that sneaky bitch has something up her sleeve." He hopped in his car and sped out the parking lot. I thought about following him and changed my mind.

The things he said hurt me and I couldn't help but wonder if what he said is true? Could Jasmine be planning to hurt my sister? I turned and looked at her getting off the floor. Nah, she ain't crazy.

****

"How have you been Teri?" I turned around and stared in the face of my ex Brian. I must admit he was still fine as hell and I couldn't erase the smile plastered on my face.

11

"I'm fine. How are you?" This is the first time I responded to him. I usually walk past but he caught me eating in the food court. Unless I'm tossing my food, I may as well respond.

"You look fine. I miss you." I put my head down.

"Look at me." He tilted my face.

"You don't feel the same?"

"I did until someone filled your spot."

"Teri, I never wanted you to leave but I understand why you did it. Just know I'll never stop loving you."

"If you told me this months ago, I probably would've asked if we could go to a room and make up for lost time. However; he came in at the right time and picked me up. I love everything about him." I noticed Shak standing there after those words left my mouth. We hadn't seen or spoken to one another since he left me at the job not too long ago.

"You don't love me anymore?"

"She said no. What part of that don't you understand?" Shakim stood in front of him with his two cousins he's always with. How the hell is Mystic even in school if he's always

12

here? I stood to throw my food out and leave. Shakim looked hella good and I wanted to fuck him all night. Knowing it wouldn't happen I decided to go home.

"I should've known you'd find a street thug."

"Excuse me." I let the tray fall out my hand and heard it slam on the table.

"I was too white for you right?" I pushed Shakim out the way since he stood toe to toe with him. I saw his fists balled up and knew one hit would knock Brian out.

"I was in love with you Brian but there's no way you felt the same because if you did, it would've never been an issue standing up for me. Hell, I protected you from your family more than you did. Why would I stay with a man scared to put his parents in their place about the foul shit they did and said to his woman."

"Teri."

"Don't you dare try and make me feel like shit for leaving a bad situation." I grabbed my stuff and went to storm off only to be stopped by this crazy bitch.

"I told you to leave him alone, didn't I?"

13

"Barb what the fuck you doing?" I heard Shakim yell behind me, as I pushed past her.

Beep! Beep! I hit the alarm on my car and sat down. I closed the door and Barb stood there smirking. I tried to open the door to get out and ask why she was watching me and it wouldn't budge.

"What the hell?"

Outta nowhere the smell of gas engulfed my car. I could see Shakim walking in my direction. I started banging on the window and saw people running over to try and open it. Something was terribly wrong. I stared down at my phone to see my mom calling. I tried to answer but the smell overwhelmed me. I began coughing and my eyes were burning.

"TERIIIIII!" Shakim and the guys started banging on the window and pulling on the door handle. Tears streamed down my face as the darkness took over. I definitely didn't think I'd die this way.

"A table for one please." I came here to get away from the BS with my sister and Meek. It seems like pain followed wherever I went and the times I ate here, were extremely peaceful.

"Right this way." The woman smiled and sat me in the exact spot Meek and I did. He must not be coming if the table is free.

"Can I start you with a drink?" I told her what I wanted and asked for the crab nachos and stuffed mushrooms for an appetizer.

She left me alone and I began staring out the window. The waves were crashing against the rocks and some men were actually surfing in this weather. It wasn't freezing but it was still cold. Yet, staring out the window kept me in a zone.

"Here's your drink." I took the red wine and sipped on it thinking about Meek. It's been a few weeks and I missed him like crazy. Not to mention, all the times I've pleasured myself with thoughts of him.

"Your appetizers miss." A guy placed them on the table. I pushed the mushrooms to the side until they cooled off. The last time, I burned my tongue really bad and felt the effects for a few days. I picked a nacho up and bit down. The sauce dripped down my face and I felt someone wiping it off.

"Meek." He smiled as he stared down at me.

"How did you know I was here?"

"I own this and everyone knows who you are. Why you think they sat you here?"

"Because you aren't here."

"Nah. They know what time it is. Can I sit?" I pointed to the other seat. Instead of sitting across, he sat directly next to me.

"I miss you ma." He turned my face to his and placed the most tender kiss on my lips. I put the wine down, sat on his lap and rested my head on his shoulder.

"I missed you so much. Meek, you don't have to love me and I'm not settling but I don't want to be without you."

"You've never been without me. I'm around, just not in your presence. I know everything you're doing." I stared at him. Why is he watching a woman he isn't with?

"Can we at least be friends? I miss talking to you and the way you call me corny."

"We could never be friends." I rose off his lap and sat in my own chair. He scooted the chair closer and took my hand in his.

"We can't be friends because I'm in love with you too. Therefore: calling one another friends isn't a good.-" I jumped on his lap again and slid his hands in my pants.

"Oh you're gonna play with my dick in front of all these people?" I turned and the place was pretty crowded.

"As long as yours is the only one I'm playing with, who cares?" His hands gripped my ass while he grinded my hips in circles on his hard dick.

"I want you so bad Meek." I sucked on his bottom lip.

"Let's go." He lifted me up, adjusted himself and told the people to wrap my food up and we'd return shortly. Well it's not exactly how he said it. His version was more of, *wrap my girl shit up and it better be done by the time I get back.*

"You are so mean."

"I'm not mean but I do need the staff to be on their feet at all times."

"If you say so. Where are we going?" He removed my shoes and had me walk on the cold sand.

"Let me show you something real quick." We stepped under the boardwalk and there was no one around. He unbuttoned his jeans, slid them and his boxers down, pulled my pants down, turned me around and pushed himself inside.

"I missed this tight, gushy pussy. Mmph."

"And I miss this big dick tearing my insides up." I held onto the boards holding the pier up and started throwing it back for him. He placed his hand around my throat and made me extremely nervous. I had to remember he likes it rough and would never intentionally hurt me.

"I love the shit outta you C." With his hand remaining around my neck, he pulled me close and tongue kissed me.

Even with my body twisted and the cold weather, nothing could bring me off this cloud he had me on

"I love you too baby. Awww shoot." I allowed my body to succumb over and over to him and once he did the same, we put our clothes on and sat there. His arms were around my waist and his chin on the top of my head.

"I wasn't sure it was lust or love which is why I didn't tell you at the time."

"It's ok Meek."

"No it's not because you left upset and I didn't even check on you and I apologize for it." I tilted my head to look at him and he pecked my lips.

"You are amazing, weird and sexy."

"I am." I had to play a little coy.

"Yup. I love how genuine and loyal you are to everyone around."

"Yea well, I wish my sister was the same." He turned my body around.

"Shak told me what happened and Teri foul as hell for it. I get she wanted to help her friend out but it shouldn't have been done at your expense. Everyone knows you two don't get along so I'm not sure why she didn't think of that."

"Am I being a baby about it? Should I be ok with it since it's her floor and I gave her free range?"

"Would you be ok with me cheating on you?" I gasped because the thought made me nauseated.

"Exactly! You learned a lot from your ex and one of the things is, you're not gonna allow anyone to walk over you again. If she's mad then tell her to buy a different building and hire whoever she wants." He held my face in his hands.

"C'Yani don't let anyone; including me make you feel bad about the choices you make. You have the right to be comfortable anywhere you go without worrying about how its gonna make the next person feel."

"I miss us talking." He smiled and hugged me tighter.

"That pussy too sore for more making up?"

"It is but I'm willing to feel the mixture of pain and pleasure again if it's coming from you."

"Good. I have a room at the Ocean Place Hilton. It's under both of our names. Go take a shower, get comfortable and I'll be there to handle that."

"Why were you staying in a room?"

"Actually, today I was coming to see and take you there. It just so happens my staff called and told me you were here."

"Really?"

"Yes really. I missed the fucked outta you C'Yani Bailey." I cheesed extremely hard. I had no idea he missed me, as much as I missed him.

"Wait! Why aren't you coming with me?"

"My pops is calling me back to back which he never does. Let me check on him and I'll be right there."

"Be careful." He carried me up the sand and walked me to the car.

"I'll see you soon." We kissed again and I pulled off. I couldn't wait until I'm lying in his arms again. You never miss a good thing until it's gone. I pushed him away but I'm glad he returned that's for sure.

****

21

"Hi my name is C'Yani Bailey and I need the key to my room." I asked the person at the front desk.

"You didn't get one when you checked in?"

"My man checked in and left the key for me."

"Oh ok. I don't mean any harm. I'm just asking because most people give the other person staying the key." The woman stared at me.

"It's fine." I wasn't giving her too much information because its none of her business and why is she asking me anyway. Who cares?

"Do you need me to show you ID?"

"No ma'am. If a person tells you their name and a key is here for them we usually give it with no questions asked."

"That doesn't seem safe." She chuckled a little.

"This hotel is very expensive and we don't get people here who aren't supposed to be. Therefore, the need to ask is unnecessary."

"Ok. I guess."

"Here is your key and per the notes on this account, your man did something very special for you."

22

"He did. Oh my God. I'm so excited. See, we broke up and just got back together. I planned on doing something nice for him but he beat me to it. I'm so sorry. I don't mean to bother you with my mess." I blurted out forgetting I just told myself not to tell her my business. I took the key and smiled.

"Honey if your man can get you this excited, then make sure you give him something special too." She smiled and pointed to the elevators.

I stepped on with excitement. I wanted to know what he did? Would I like it? How did he get it done so fast? It's all a mystery and I couldn't wait to slide the key in the door. Once I did, my eyes grew wide. There were bags from Gucci, Prada, Giuseppe, Louboutin and others.

I shop in these stores here and there but never had this much stuff at one time. I looked in a few and there were shoes, purses, clothes and I noticed a card on the bed.

"To the woman who opened my eyes to a whole other world. You are truly special and I don't ever plan on letting you go. I love your bougie, non-fighting but can fuck me good

ass. This is just the beginning C'Yani and I can't wait to spoil you even more.

I put the card down and started crying. All these years wasted on Ty and God finally placed a good man in front of me. Crazy, hood and aggressive but good to me.

I stood and went in the bathroom to find rose petals at the bottom. When I turned the water on they began to float. There was soft music playing and a tv in the wall where the tub was. Oh yes, this is an expensive hotel.

After my bath, I threw on a hotel robe and laid on the bed. The news was on and I dosed off, only to wake up to a presence next to me.

"Meek!"

"Nope." I couldn't tell the voice and jumped up.

"Who are you and..." I stopped after noticing something on the other side of the room. It was another person. Is this part of the surprise Meek had for me? When I saw the bat, my eyes grew wide and all I kept praying was for Meek to make it here in time to save me.

"I'm pulling up now." I told my grandfather on the phone. He asked if I heard from my father because he was supposed to stop by and its not like him to do a no show.

I was shocked because he had been calling my phone back to back and it's not like him. Unfortunately, I was making love to my woman under the boardwalk so I couldn't answer. I told him I was here and would have my father call.

I stepped out my truck with a smile on my face thinking about C'Yani. I was happy to be in her presence and becoming a couple again. I know it sounds corny but she had a way of making me do corny things with her. She's the calm to any storm I endure.

"What up?" I walked in and instantly became pissed seeing Kim sitting at the table. She had a grin on her face, which means the bitch is up to no good. The real question is, why is she here?

"Tha fuck you doing here?" She came to me and ran her hand up and down my chest. I grabbed her wrist and bent them back.

"Bitch, don't play with me. Why you here and where's my pops?"

"He's outta commission right now." I dropped her hands and started searching the house for him.

"Outta commission?" I was confused.

"Let me show you." I followed her upstairs and found my father lying in bed with handcuffs around his arms and legs. His eyes were closed and I could see him barely breathing. He was covered but you could tell he may have been naked.

"Now we're gonna be together." She's still delusional as fuck.

"Pops, you ok?" I ran to him but her words stopped me.

"You see that bitch you fell for is cheating on you." She opened a phone and I heard someone moaning.

"Your bitch ain't thinking about you." She turned the phone and there was C'Yani in a video riding Ty. I'm assuming it's him because she ain't the type to sleep around.

"That shit could be old."

"I don't think so." I snatched the phone out her hands and I'll be damned. There sat the bags I brought her in front of the bed.

"And you left me for her." I was livid because not only did we just fuck, how the hell she fucking another nigga in the hotel room I rented? I couldn't wait to get my hands on her. I wasn't gonna let Kim know how bad it hurt to see that shit and changed the subject.

"Why the fuck you got my pops handcuffed?" I looked around for the keys.

"I wanted to see if he could fuck me as good as you." I snapped my neck to look at her.

"What the fuck you say?" I tried to remove the handcuffs but she had the keys jiggling in her hand.

"You heard me."

"Hold the fuck up! You fucked my pops?" She had a smile on her face like it was cute.

"He definitely has a big dick and made me cum a few times but his touch isn't like yours." I took my gun out and shot the bedpost to let his arms down.

"Pops you ok?" I smacked his face a few times to wake up. His eyes opened and he had a sad look.

"You have to kill her." He managed to get out and she heard him.

"That's why you're in the position you're in. Do you know your father called me crazy while I was riding him? Oh but he wasted no time cumming inside me. Meek you and I are gonna be pregnant because I'm ovulating and..." I turned and took a shot. I only got her in the arm and went to shoot again but my father called me.

"I need an ambulance." I had no idea what he was talking about because he looked fine. It wasn't until I moved the covers and he had what appeared to be stab wounds all over his body.

"SHIT!!!!" I call 911 quick and found some towels to keep the blood from pouring out. The comforter was so dark, I never noticed the blood.

"Hang on pops. They're coming." As bad as I wanted to get that bitch I couldn't because the 911 operator told me to apply pressure until the EMT's arrived.

29

"Meeeeeeekkkkkkkk. How can you shoot me? What if our baby got hurt?" I ignored her and pressed down as hard as I could to try my best at making sure he didn't die.

"Ahhhhh fuckkkkk!" I felt something sharp being impounded in my back.

"Bitch, are you fucking crazy?" I stood and used every bit of energy I had to strangle her. Whatever she left in my back, went in further as she kicked me in the nuts and pushed me against the wall, to get me off.

"Look what you made me do." I could hear the ambulance or some sirens in the distance.

"I'll be back to check on you baby. I need to get this bullet out my shoulder and check on our baby." She kissed my lips and shortly after my eyes closed. If I make it outta here alive, I'm gonna kill her and C'Yani.

After Meek barged in my home, slammed me in to the wall, tossed me on the ground and threatened me, it has been my mission to destroy C'Yani Bailey. I have nothing but hatred towards that woman and I want her to go down. She needs to lose everything just to bring her stuck up ass back to reality.

C'Yani is one of those women who think because she had a career, high position, own place and money to blow, she's better than the rest of us. She went to college and so did I, but you don't see me walking around with my nose in the air. Shit, her and Teri were raised together and she isn't anywhere near the same. She's down to earth and has no problem taking up for me or including me in her new endeavors. Hell, its what best friends are supposed to do for one another.

I was happy as hell when Teri offered me an office on her floor. I hadn't used my degree and really didn't plan on it but if someone offered me something to better myself, of course I'm going to take it. The only thing is, when her sister found out, she wasn't happy and neither was her boyfriend.

31

They each had something to say, which made my best friend change her mind and offer to help me find a new spot.

It was at that moment, I decided to make it my mission to get rid of her. That's why when I ran into Mia, who is Kim's sister, I devised a plan to sabotage C'Yani and Meek's relationship and if she died in the process, it's not my problem.

See Mia and I went to school together and lost contact after graduation. We ran into one another and ended up seeing C'Yani out. Mia explained how Shak kicked her out C'Yani's house after she went to ask for her job back through her. Again, he was becoming a problem as well, so when she mentioned him having a ho house, I remembered Barb, who used to strip lived there. Yup, I called her up and she was pissed Teri had him throw her out and won't return her calls or text messages. She stopped by and we stayed at my house that night coming up with all types of ways to get C'Yani and Teri.

Yes, Teri's my best friend but I couldn't stand her man and if Barb could get him away from her, we'd be fine. I'm not saying Teri's going to get hurt because it isn't what I wanted but Barb said, it had to be some sort of accident proven to be done by her, so she wouldn't want to be bothered with him any longer. In her head, he'd confront her about it and she'd seduce him.

We all know a woman is not going to stick around a man with a bunch of drama. As far as C'Yani goes, Meek deserves to feel pain after hurting myself and Ty, which is why this plan is perfect.

"You sure about this Jasmine?" Mia asked as we took the employee stairs up to the room Meek rented. Evidently, Kim had been following him for quite some time and keeping her distance. After the shit she told me, the bitch is certified crazy and delusional. She says he won't hurt her, but I'm not sure if he tossed her out of a moving truck. The only reason she didn't get run over is because it was late and someone found her. She had a lot of fractured body parts but her persistent ass refused to stay put.

"I'm positive." I sent a text message to Ty, telling him to meet me here in an hour and what room number I'm at. I was hoping C'Yani would be here before Meek because if not, we'd be stuck.

"The guy gave you the key right?" I asked about the manager she was sleeping with. When we devised the plan, she started asking questions and him not knowing, answered each one.

"Not really. He has an extra card so I took it."

"What if he notices that it's gone?"

"Girl please. He went out last night and hungover like crazy. When he gets like that, he'll sleep until the next day. We can do whatever and I'll return the key without him knowing."

"Are you sure Kim said this is the hotel?"

"I told you she has a tracking device on his truck and he came here. She saw him go the desk and tell the woman he was leaving a key for the chick. Trust me. We got this." I nodded and couldn't help but think about how crazy her sister really is. Meek is definitely someone you'd wanna stay fucking with but she's doing way too much.

BEEP! The door opened and both of our mouths dropped staring at all the bags he had. Name brand shit and I know for a fact he had to spend thousands on the items. We began going through it without taking much out and a bitch was jealous as hell.

I saw Mia look down at her phone, grin and then tell me its time. It only meant her sister mentioned Meek being on the way to her for the shit she had going on, which means C'Yani is on her way up. We put the black masks on our face, hid in the closet and waited.

The door beeped and you could hear her gasp and run over to the bags. She checked in some of the bags, and the shoes she pulled out were bad. I had to remember which ones so I could take them. He can buy her more, well if he even deals with her once we're done.

She started the bath water after looking and Mia wanted to drown her but that would be too easy. The bitch needed to suffer so we waited and luckily, we did because she dosed off. It gave us time to get ourselves together to finish this out. She must've felt our presence because she woke up.

"Meek!" She woke up when the two of us were standing on the side of the bed.

"Nope!" Mia spoke because I didn't need her linking me to this shit. Teri would never forgive me and believe it or not, I value our friendship.

"Who are you?" She backed up on the bed. Terror was written on her face and it gave me great pleasure to punch her in it.

"AHHHHHHH." She screamed out and Mia looked at me.

"Shut the fuck up." Mia shouted. We jumped on the bed and continued beating the shit outta her. Mia had a bat and started hitting her in the legs and arms.

The only reason we stopped is because someone knocked on the door. I stared down at C'Yani and her face was covered in blood, her arm appeared to be broken and she had to be unconscious or dead because she wasn't moving.

"We have to get her in the other room." Mia and I each grabbed an ankle, drug her off the bed and heard her head hit the ground.

"What about the covers?" Mia pointed to the comforter full of blood and helped me rush to get it off the bed, along with her clothes. I told her to take them in the other room and stay until she hears me executing the next part of the plan. I took all my clothes off, and went to the door naked.

"Damn baby." Ty grabbed my waist and pulled me in for a kiss.

"You know I prefer to be naked at all times for you."

"And I appreciate it." I closed the door, led him to the bed and pushed him down. I'm not sure when Meek would be returning, so this had to be done fast. I stripped him out his clothes and climbed on top.

"Ssssss. Jasmine. Shittttt." I had my lower half grinding on his rock hard dick.

"You feel good Jas." His arms were around my waist and I noticed Mia peeking out the room. I waved for her to come out since his eyes were closed and had her record me from behind. Meek won't know the difference, especially with my hair the same color and length as C'Yani's. The bags would be a dead giveaway too.

"I'm about to cum." Ty moaned out and I caught an attitude.

"Already. What the hell?"

"Jas, you know I haven't had any sex so cut the shit. We can fuck again right after. Oh fuckkkkk." He shot his load in me and I hopped off to throw my clothes on.

"Jasmine don't be mad. You know I can fuck all night."

"Whatever. I don't even feel like being here anymore."

"What? This hotel is nice as shit. Let's go take a bath or fuck on the balcony." He stood and tried to go in the bathroom but I stopped him. I'm not sure if the bitch left anything in there and I couldn't take the chance of him noticing any of her stuff. They've been together for five years. It would be stupid of me to believe he didn't know her scent or something.

"Yea well, I'm turned off now. So let's go."

"Really Jas?" I had to hurry up and get outta here because it's no telling when he's coming. He sucked his teeth, put his clothes on and followed me out the door. I sent a text to Mia and told her to come out with some of the bags. Hell yea I'm keeping some of that shit. I won't wear it around anyone but I'm keeping it for sure.

"Who are they?" Ty pointed to a few guys jumping out a truck and rushing into the building as we were getting in the car.

"I have no idea." I looked again and almost shit on myself when I noticed the crazy cousin with the eyes, two older men and two other younger dudes. It was another guy but I couldn't see who he was because of how fast he ran inside. I know damn well they not here for her. Oh well if they are. I wish I could see their faces when they get to her.

"They seem to be looking for someone. Whoever it is better run because they don't seem to be in a good mood." I said goodbye and went to my car. I waited for Mia to exit the hotel and felt relieved when she did holding a bunch of bags. The bitch must've taken some for herself.

"You coming over?" Ty's voice boomed through my Bluetooth when I answered.

"I guess."

"Come on Jas. I'll definitely make it worth your while."

"You better." I hung up and dialed Mia.

"Bitch are you sure the cameras were turned off throughout the hotel?" I became nervous after seeing them because once they find C'Yani, I know for a fact they'll go straight to the office looking for the tapes.

"Yes, bitch. He told me how to use the timer and what they do when niggas creep or some shit. They turn back on in an hour so we good." I felt better. We didn't plan this shit out for weeks to mess up and get caught.

"Alright and don't be tryna keep the stuff I picked out." She busted out laughing and hung up. That bitch better not play with me.

I drove to Ty's house to finish what we started. I hated to get up afterwards but we had to get out of there. I can't wait for Meek to see the video. Whether he fucks me again or not, he won't be with her and it's all that matters.

"Fuck! Think Shakim. Think." I said to myself pacing outside Teri's car. In the short amount of time we've known one another, I fell in love with this woman and I'm not about to let her die already.

Everyone was still banging on the window tryna get her out. Seconds felt like hours and time was of the essence. Some man had a crowbar tryna open it but it didn't work. I saw the tears rolling down her face and the way she begged for help. My heart was breaking because not only is the gas smell strong, it also smelled like something was burning, which means I had to hurry up. Then it dawned on me what to do.

"MOVE!" I pulled my gun out, aimed it at the back window and shot. The window didn't shatter right away.

"What the hell type of windows are these?" Lil Faz asked. I continued shooting and eventually the glass shattered. You could smell the gas stench and everyone jumped back. I opened the back door, reached to open the front and for some reason it wouldn't budge.

41

"The door is stuck. Shit." I jumped out, ran to the passenger side and reached for her.

"Faz, shoot the window." I was coughing hard from the smell and needed to release the seatbelt on the other side of her but I couldn't reach it.

"What if I hit her?"

"Be careful."

POW! POW!

"FUCK!" Blood began pouring out her leg because the bullet ricocheted and hit her. He reached inside and undid the seatbelt.

Once I pulled her out, cops, ambulances and fire trucks pulled up. I could barely breathe and Teri appeared to be dead. I lost it when they tried to take her outta my arms. I'll say it again, I am madly in love with this woman and I'm not about to lose her. Faz had to make me let go so she could get to the hospital.

"MOVEEEEE!!! IT'S GONNA BLOWWWWW!" Someone shouted and I felt people pulling me away.

BOOM! The explosion was so loud it left ringing in my ear and the ground shook. A few cars exploded with it because they were close.

"You ok sir?" I nodded my head and asked for Teri.

"She's in route to the hospital. Put this on your face." The woman placed an oxygen mask on and just that fast, it felt better. My cousin stared at me as he spoke on the phone. He's most likely informing the family which is one last thing I have to do. I already know shit is gonna hit the fan.

"We need to get you checked out." I stood and let them put me in the ambulance. I laid back thinking of ways to kill Barb. She assumed I didn't see her and I may not have if Teri wouldn't have made eye contact with her. I think its Teri's way of telling me who's responsible.

****

"Are you ok?" I heard and looked to see my parents and siblings. I ended up falling asleep in the ambulance.

"How is she?" I threw my legs off to stand.

"We don't know yet."

"How long has it been?"

43

"Not long."

"Shit! I have to get outta here." I went to use the bathroom and came out to see Fazza, Mazza, and my great uncle.

"I'm fine. Why are all of you here?" I asked and they had sad looks on their faces.

"Something happened to Meek, and James. We also can't find C'Yani."

"What happened to my cousins?"

"Someone stabbed them and were not sure if either are going to make it." Fazza said.

"We've been trying to reach C'Yani but she's not answering." Ty chimed in.

"WHATTTTT?" I started pacing the hospital room. This couldn't be happening right now. The niggas we looking for haven't even caused this much ruckus.

"He was with her at his restaurant and reserved a room for them. Did anyone check there?"

"Which hotel?" Mazza asked and when I told him, he left with one of his sons that came, lil Faz, Fazza and Mystic.

44

Everyone knew how Meek felt about C, and if anything happened he's gonna have a fit because we didn't check on her.

"Who did this?" My mom wasted no time asking.

"Barb."

"Barb?" Everyone shouted. They knew she's one of the women from my ho house. They never met her or any of the chicks I slept with because they were fuck buddies. But everyone is aware of the way I lived.

Shit, my cousin Fazza is the one who put me up on the ho house. He said, *if you ain't got no bitch and love fucking other women, why not have them in a house to fuck on demand?* I thought he was bugging at first but when Mazza told me it was true, I asked questions. And not too long after, did what he said and made sure they stayed clean.

If they slept with other men, I had a doctor come over and re test them. Condoms are good but I'm extra careful. I've even allowed other men to come by with chicks and fuck them there. I didn't give a fuck and all the women knew it. They all tried to do what Teri did and that's get me to settle down but each one failed. I don't know what it is about her but she definitely has my heart.

"She hates Teri because I kicked her out and she got her ass beat. Man, I didn't know she was even capable of anything like this."

"What did she do?" I began explaining and each of them were shocked. My mom stood in front of me and kept asking if I were ok. My sister was crying and Shawn appeared to be nervous too. All the time I've been in the streets, nothing like this has ever happened to me. They always say women are more dangerous than men, and in this case, it's true.

"Ok. let's check on Meek and my son." My uncle looked distraught.

"Shakim, they want you to get a chest X-ray to make sure no smoke is in your lungs."

"Another time. I need to check on..."

"You need to go Shakim. We can't take the chance of you passing out because you didn't listen." Shawn said and came with me to the radiology department. I could tell he was nervous about my health just like everyone else so I went to appease them. In my eyes, I'm fine but you never know.

"How's my cousins?" I wasted no time asking as we waited for the tech to come get me.

"I'm not sure Shakim. We got a call saying you were hurt and rushed up here."

"Who called?"

"One of those ho's." I busted out laughing and went to get the X-ray done. Evidently, they did one when I first arrived and my lungs were dark or some shit. The doctor wanted to make sure they're cleared up.

"You good?"

"I guess. The guy didn't say anything." Shawn nodded and the two of us walked out the radiology department.

After the quick x-ray, I had Shawn drive me to the hotel as well. It's no way I could face Meek and not have an answer for the question we all know he'd ask. My cousin finally admitted to himself he was in love with her and felt the need to do whatever and win her back.

We pulled up at the same time my cousins did. Evidently, the GPS took them out the way. I ran over to the receptionist desk and asked which room his name was under and requested a key. Once the bitch told me no, I jumped behind the counter, grabbed the key she had which most likely went to every room and all of us ran up the stairs except lil Faz. He stayed to make sure she didn't contact the police.

"C'YANI!" I shouted when the door opened. The bed was unmade and the comforter was missing. I didn't think anything of it and searched the room with everyone else.

"OH SHIT! CALL 911!" I heard Mazza yell and we all ran to where he was. C'Yani laid on the floor in just a robe, a bloody face and unconscious.

"Meek is gonna fucking lose it." Fazza said and placed the call. Ten minutes later cops and EMT's swarmed the room asking us questions. My stepfather spoke since he knew two of them and requested to see the video tape. Whoever did this tried to kill her or something. The way she looked is like a scene out of a movie.

48

"Excuse us." The EMT's shouted and rushed out with C. All of us searched for the bags and nothing. He told me about the shopping spree he went on for her and couldn't wait to see her face when she saw them.

"Where's the bags?" Fazza asked and I shrugged my shoulders.

"You think it was a robbery?" Mystic questioned and Mazza checked the door.

"Nah. Whoever did it knew her or him. There's no sign of a break in." He pointed to the door that had no kick marks or anything. We all glanced at each other.

"KIM!" All of us shouted and left out to find out about the surveillance video. Every hotel has one. By the time we got down there, Shawn and lil Faz had somber looks on their faces.

"What happened?"

"The video was placed on a timer, which means there's no footage. Whoever did this planned it out perfect because the video is set to go back on in another ten minutes." Shawn said.

"How the hell is that even possible?"

"The person had to know someone or paid a high-tech individual to break in the system and do it."

"SHIT!" Fazza had his hands on top of his head and Mazza was on the phone with his tech guy tryna find out if he could hack into the system and get any information.

"We need to get back to the hospital." I walked out with everyone behind me.

"Who's gonna tell Meek?" Shawn asked and I continued staring out the window.

"Mazza is the calmest and will probably be the one because I damn sure ain't." The rest of the ride was quiet.

We pulled up at the hospital and my first stop was to see Meek and James. Both of them were stabbed but his dad suffered more. Whoever got to them, stabbed Meek in the back and dug so deep it punctured a lung. His dad had multiple stab wounds to the chest and abdomen and they weren't sure if he were going to make it because of the massive amount of blood loss. Shawn said the doctor told them they were gonna do their best but to pray for a miracle.

"How are they?" I asked my mom.

"Where the hell did you go?" She snapped and everyone looked.

"You do know I'm grown right?" She came over to me.

"Shakim the doctor said your x-rays were fine and you could go home but he had no way of contacting you. Then I call and you don't answer. I thought you passed out or something and they weren't able to tell me." I could see worry in her face but she should've known Shawn would've told her. I let it go because she has the ability to piss me off and I'm not tryna be more stressed out.

"We had to check on C'Yani."

"Teri's parents came looking for you." I didn't miss her ignoring me saying we had to check on C. My mom wasn't feeling her because the day she came over to meet the family, C'Yani didn't like the way my great uncle spoke to her and said something. My mother felt she was being disrespectful.

It's always something with her and I think it's because Mazza and Fazza still don't fuck with her. She hasn't been the same since but it's her fault and she always finds a way to take her anger out on people who have nothing to do with it.

"I'll go see her when I check on Meek."

"Meek is fine but his dad is still in surgery. Go check on Teri and don't leave this hospital again." I waved her off and walked out. I hated when she forgot my age.

"Ma. Daddy." I woke up expecting to see my parents and instead saw Shakim. Not that it was a problem but where were they.

"I'm glad you woke up." He leaned down and placed a kiss on my lips. I don't know why but I busted out crying.

"You in pain?" He stood and pressed the button for the nurse to come.

"Is everything ok?"

"Yea my girl woke up and I think she's in pain." I attempted to move and noticed a huge brace on my leg.

"Lil Faz accidently shot you when we were tryna get you out. Well, he didn't directly shoot you. The bullet ricocheted off the window but it was the only way we could get you out." I nodded and watched the doctor step in. I did smile a little knowing him and his cousin are the reason I'm still breathing,

"I'll be right back." I didn't say anything as he held the phone to his ear and barked at whoever it was.

"Ms. Bailey, how are you feeling?"

"Fine." I tried to move again and the pain was excruciating.

"How long have I been here?" The doctor began doing vitals.

"A few hours. We had to operate and take the bullet out your leg but were you aware of the pregnancy?" When he mentioned me being pregnant, the look of shock had to be evident on my face. Granted, I knew the consequences but damn.

"Yea, you're about six weeks." I got pregnant the day we had sex the first time. I mean we been around each other much longer but he wasn't playing when he said, he was making sure I got pregnant.

"I want to check you." He pulled the stethoscope from around his neck and asked the nurse to bring in the ultrasound machine.

"WAIT!" I shouted and put my hand out.

"Can we wait until he leaves?" He gave me a weird look.

"I'm not sure if he's the father and it will be a lot of problems if he finds out." I had to think of a quick lie because the doctor wasn't tryna hear it.

"Ms. Bailey, we have to make sure the child is ok."

"How did you know I was pregnant in the first place?" I tried to catch an attitude because Shakim is bound to walk in.

"We ran your blood work and when we found out, I had to do an ultrasound in the operating room. I want to check now that you're awake to make sure the child is ok. Don't you want to see the baby?"

"I do and I will. Let me get rid of him first please." The look on his face was unsure and the nurse had the same one.

"If either of you spill this information, I promise to sue the hospital." I'm not even sure why I decided to hide this from him anyway.

"Ma'am, we'd never do that. There's guidelines for…"

"I know the protocol and it's been known for people to release it anyway."

"Ms. Bailey, I will never disclose this but he needs to go now so we can check."

55

"Ok. Can you help me in the bathroom and I'll do it?" The nurse did like I asked and assisted me. I washed my face, and cleaned myself up the best I could with a brace on. When I came out Shakim was in the chair watching television. He stood and carried me over to the bed. I nodded at the nurse to let her know I'm about to do it. She closed the door and I asked Shak to sit on the bed.

"I'm so happy you made it. Babe, I have something to tell you." I saw the love he had in his eyes for me, which made what I'm about to say harder.

"Me first. Shak, I love you so much and its hurting me to say this."

"Say what because it better not be you breaking up with me." The tears started falling down my face.

"Shakim its obvious the woman is going to continue attacking me for being with you and I can't be around it."

"She's about to die Teri so you have nothing to worry about."

"What about the other women you sleep with? Huh? What if they wake up one day and want you the same way?

56

The Tasha bitch is her friend and seems to feel the same as she does. What if it happens again? I can't worry about who's gonna attack me every time I leave the house."

"Teri, we're not breaking up."

"Shakim listen to me. I don't wanna be without you but I've never dealt with any drama in my life like this. Then my ex came…"

"You tryna tell me you want that mothafucka?" I, in no way shape or form will ever be with Brian again but maybe if I say yes, he'll leave me alone. But then again, I'm a little nervous about his response. I tried my luck anyway and wished I didn't.

"Maybe. I mean he did say he still wanted me and…" His hand gripped my hair tight, and my neck felt like it would snap.

"I understand you're upset but ain't nobody ever gonna bed you again and I fucking mean it."

"Let go Shak." His grip got tighter.

"You heard what the fuck I said. I wish you would be with some nigga." He slammed my head against the pillow and stood.

"Shakim how could you put your hands on me?" My neck was hurting due to the way he yanked it.

"Be happy that's all I did because I really wanna choke the shit outta you." He stood and his hands were on top of his head. The way he paced back and forth made me more nervous because he was snapping.

"Do you love me Teri?" I tried wiping the tears but they were coming full speed.

"Just go Shakim."

"You are the first woman I ever loved and you know this. Is this a game to you? Did you make me fall, to see if you could?"

"Shakim, I didn't even know about that until we slept together the first time."

"It don't even matter at this point. I could force you to be with me but why? You wanna fuck someone else, be my guest."

"I don't wanna sleep with anyone else Shakim."

"I always thought you'd be the woman I'd marry and have kids with but I won't be with a woman who can't weather a storm, I didn't even know existed." He grabbed his keys and phone.

"You're telling me you'd stick around after someone attacked you over me?"

"You can't control what a mothafucka does, therefore; I couldn't fault you for what he did. Would I leave you? No because my heart belongs to only you and unless you cheated nothing could take me away. But I see now."

"See what?"

"You're blaming me for what she did and I get it. But I didn't tell her to do no shit like that and if I even assumed she'd fuck with you, I wouldn't even think twice about ending her."

"Shak, please understand."

"I don't have to understand shit but I want you to understand this." He stood directly next to me and put his hand behind my head and pulled me closer.

"The second I walk out that door we are through. Don't call me, text, drop by or even speak if we cross paths."

"Shakim."

"You will always have a place in my heart Teri and that's some real shit but you don't want me. I can force you to be with me, but I refuse to see you unhappy, regardless of how you're making me feel."

"I don't want…" He shushed me with his lips.

"I'll always love you Teri." He kissed my forehead and left me crying my eyes out. I screamed for him to return because after listening to him, I realized he couldn't control what she did. I know he's gonna find her and maybe I shouldn't have jumped the gun.

"SHAKKKKK!" I screamed again and nothing. I fell back on the pillow and picked my phone up to call. His phone went straight to voicemail, which means he either blocked me or shut it off. *What did I do?*

****

"You are six weeks like I told you previously." I cried staring at my child on the screen. I don't know why I sent

60

Shakim home when he had the right to be here. I know if he knew about this child he wouldn't leave me alone. Now I'm lying here crying my eyes out because I want him here but he still hasn't taken me off block or shut his phone on, whichever is the case. It's not like I can leave and tell him because of the what happened. The doctor advised me to stay for a few days.

"I'm gonna give you a two-week supply of pre-natal vitamins. It should be more than enough time to set up an appointment with a gynecologist and let him or her give you a full prescription." I nodded and stared as he disconnected the machine after handing me a picture.

"Ms. Bailey, I don't know what the situation is with the man who left and if it's another but it's also not fair to keep this a secret."

"Excuse me."

"I don't want to cause you any aggravation but if a woman were possibly carrying my child, I'd still want to know. Women think men don't care about the process but a lot of them do and want to be there. Think about that."

61

"Think about what? Honey are you ok and where's Shakim?" My mom asked and the doctor stared at me.

"He left." I turned over and snatched the picture but not fast enough.

"OH MY GOD! I'M GONNA BE A GRANDMA AGAIN!" She shouted and my father smiled. I took the picture out her hand.

"I'm not keeping it?"

"The hell you not. Teri, we did not raise you to be a woman to terminate your child. Now if you don't wish to keep it, I'm sure Shakim will." My father barked.

"Teri, you're being unfair to him. Yes, it's your body but the child belongs to both of you."

"It is my body and I'm the one who has to deliver. What if the same thing happens to me, that happened to C'Yani? I may be strong but I don't know if I could be that strong." My mom sat on the bed and hugged me.

The reason I didn't want a child is because I still wanted to travel. I was also deathly scared of losing it or having a stillborn like my sister. We couldn't wait for my nephew to grace this world and when she lost it, my ass cried as if it were my own child. Then to know the father stressed her out and is most likely the reason, is scary. What if Shakim's whores found out and made the pregnancy worse? The stress alone would make me miscarry.

"Teri don't use what happened to C'Yani as the reason you don't want your child." She lifted my face and wiped my tears.

"Shakim loves you and anyone on the outside looking in, knows that. Honey, you and C'Yani found men who worship the ground you walk on. Don't let that man miss out on a miracle because you're scared."

"I broke up with him and he told me not to contact him ever again."

"I bet he did. Teri you told me he let you know you're the first woman he's ever loved. You love him with all you had to make him feel secure, only to leave him alone. I wouldn't wanna be bothered either." My father had an attitude like I broke up with him.

"I don't wanna walk around paranoid about his past."

63

"Teri everyone has a past and no one can predict what any of the people in them will come do, or try to win them back. He had no idea she'd do that and instead of seeing how he'd handle the situation you broke up with him. It's going to take a lot to win him back." I continued crying on my mother's shoulder when two policemen stepped in.

"Are you Mr. and Mrs. Bailey?"

"Yes." They had sad looks on their faces.

"We need for you to come identify a woman we think may be your daughter."

"WHAT!" My father jumped up.

"A woman was brought in two hours ago and we've been trying to find her parents. We've been to your house and even waited but we couldn't find you. It wasn't until one of the nurses told our colleague a woman with the same last name is here and could possibly be related."

"Where's my daughter?" My mom ran to the door and they kept her in.

"She's coming out of surgery but I want to tell you, whoever attacked her…"

"ATTACKED!" We all shouted.

"Yes, someone brutally attacked her and had no one found her she may not be here." I covered my mouth crying.

"I'm coming." I pressed the button for the nurse and asked for a wheelchair. There's no way they're going without me.

After they placed me in a wheelchair, we followed the cops down to the room C'Yani would be placed in, which is on the ICU floor. We all knew if you're on this floor it's because you either suffered a lotta trauma or they're hiding you. The cops did tell us they'd have security at her door.

Evidently, the person or persons who did this were able to tap into the video camera and cut it off for a few hours. They have no idea who did it or why. Supposedly, Meek was going to meet her so they're unsure if the attack was meant for her or him. Whatever the case, once the nurses wheeled her in, all of us cried. Her face was covered in bandages besides her eyes.

The doctor said her nose is bruised and her jaw is fractured but not where they had to wire it shut. Her arm is broken and both of her eyes are swollen shut. She has a very bad concussion and small swelling on the brain they're keeping an eye on. Two teeth on the side of her mouth are gone and she has bruised ribs. I was at a loss for words.

All I could think of is who on earth would wanna hurt her? For a quick second I thought of Jasmine but she values our friendship too much to harm her. Is this what Shakim tried to tell me before I cut him off? I guess I'll never know because he isn't speaking to me.

"How's my father?" I asked the moment my eyes opened. My entire family was sitting there which had me nervous.

"He's in ICU."

"I'm gonna kill that bitch." I attempted to get up but the pain was too bad.

"Meek, you were stabbed deep. The knife punctured your lung." My grandmother stood on the side of me.

"I have to get outta here."

"I know you're grown but not tonight." I could argue with her but decided against it. She's known not to give a fuck and will probably smack me.

"Meek, we have to tell you something." Zia walked over with a sad look on her face.

"What? Is my cousin ok?"

"Shakim is fine. When's the last time you saw C'Yani?"

"Fuck that bitch!" They all gave me a crazy look. Thinking about her fucking that nigga triggered my anger and I couldn't wait to see her. She better hope I don't kill her.

"I'm not sure why you're saying that but..."

"No disrespect Zia but I don't wanna know shit about her."

"Meek she's..." My grandmother tried to speak and I cut her off too.

"I don't give a fuck where she is. Don't tell her where I'm at or allow her next to me. Matter of fact, don't mention her around me ever again."

"Cuz, something happened to her." Lil Faz tried to tell me.

"I don't care if the bitch dies. Don't mention her around me." Nobody else said a word and sat there in silence.

"I wanna see my father."

"I'll take him." Fazza said and helped me out the bed. Everyone else said their goodbyes except his wife and kids. They came with us.

"What happened to you?" I noticed Teri in a wheelchair sitting outside one of the rooms.

"It's a long story. You here to see C'Yani?"

"Why the fuck would I do that? She can stay with her ex. I don't give a fuck."

"What are you taking about? She's..." I put my hand up for her to be quiet and saw my family shaking their heads. I know they all loved C but too bad because she and I are over.

"You ain't shit nigga. How the fuck you gonna leave her like this?" I snapped my neck.

"I don't know what happened with him and your cousin but he's adamant on not discussing her. He won't listen to anything regarding her." Ty told her.

"WHATTTTTTTT? She needs you and you're walking away? I'll make sure to let her know. Stupid ass nigga."

"Fuck you and her."

"It's like that? Ok. Don't bring your stupid ass around when you find out the truth either. She's not going to forgive you."

69

"Nah Teri. I'm never gonna forgive her." I asked Fazza to push me in my dad's room because I'm finished going back and forth with her.

We stepped in and my father had the oxygen tube in his nose. Monitors were on his body but I'm not sure where because he's covered up. I lifted the blanket and noticed the bandages on his chest and stomach. Fazza said, the doctor told them he had over twenty stab wounds and a few were deep. If I didn't get there in time he would've been dead. All I could think of is killing Kim. I should've done it a long time ago but she stayed away. In my mind she wasn't a threat to me. Yet; she found a way to get me anyway and that's through my father.

My grandfather was lying in the chair as my grandmother came out the bathroom with a washcloth to clean my father's face off. She claims he had sleep in his eyes. He isn't in a coma and can wake up whenever but I think she wanted to feel like she's helping. It's not much you can do when a person is in a situation such as this.

"He's gonna be fine. Who did this?" I hated to answer her.

"Kim."

"KIM!"

"Yea. Pops called for me to stop by. I get there and she's in the kitchen waiting for me. Long story short, Pops was handcuffed to the bed and she had sex with him."

"Tha fuck?" Fazza's face and everyone else's was turned up.

"She said, him cumming inside her will plant a seed for us to have a child. I shot her in the arm and when I went to strangle her, she kicked me in the nuts and pushed me against the wall making the knife go in deeper. The bitch screamed out asking how I can almost kill her with our baby in her stomach."

"Yo the bitch has to go." Fazza was just as angry as the rest of us. I know its bothering him and Mazza because they're in Delaware and all of us are here. I won't be surprised if they move back to be closer.

"I know. I only got her in the arm because Pops was dying and I needed to apply pressure."

"Meek ain't nobody questioning your actions." I wiped the lone tear falling down my face. Hell yea I'm crying over him. I don't know if I could take losing two parents.

"My aim ain't never been off. She kept moving and..." My grandfather put his hand on my shoulder.

"Don't carry that weight grandson. No one could've predicted anything she did. You and my son are ok and it's all that matters." I nodded and stared at my father take slow breaths. At least he's alive.

****

It's been two and a half weeks since the stabbing and shockingly C'Yani hasn't called or text. I guess she's enjoying her time with the ex. Here I was scared about revealing my true feelings because of her going back to him and she did it anyway.

I thought about driving to her parents' house because Shak told me she left her sisters and decided to go home after the bullshit with Jasmine, but changed my mind. I didn't

72

wanna hear her admit to being with him and then killing her.

I'll see her eventually but right now I needed rest.

I parked in my driveway and noticed Shak's car. I

didn't bother walking over to it because he had a key, which

meant he's inside. I opened the door and he and my other

cousins were playing the game. He saw me and passed the

controller off.

"What up cuz?"

"Shit."

"We need to talk." He walked up the steps with me.

"About?" I've seen him since waking up and he hadn't

said anything about having a conversation. I mean we spoke on

the shit with Barb and Teri breaking up with him but nothing

concerning me. I could see how hard he took it on Teri leaving

him and didn't wanna badger him about it. A breakup is hard

and people have to deal with it in their own way.

"What the fuck is up with you not going to visit

C'Yani?"

"I'm good on her."

"Meek, I'm your favorite cousin, your best friend nigga and I know shit ain't good with you." I sat on my bed.

"She went back to fucking him." I blew my breath out and stared at the ceiling.

"Damn."

"That's why I don't wanna talk about it. You of all people knew my struggle with coming clean about my feelings." He shook his head.

"I wanna kill both of them for tryna play me."

"I agree but let me ask you this." He lit a blunt and took a pull.

"You think he did that to her?"

"Did what?" I was confused.

"Oh shit. I forgot you refused to listen when everyone tried to tell you." He sat on the dresser in my room.

"Tell me what?" He had a sad look on his face.

"Cuz, someone attacked her in the hotel room."

"WHATTTT!" I jumped up off the bed and began pacing. Who the hell would fight her? She doesn't bother anyone.

"I thought you didn't care."

"I don't. What happened?" He laughed.

"If you don't care, why would I tell you?" He got a kick outta the way I acted and thinking back, maybe I should've listened.

"Nigga stop playing." I snatched the blunt.

"I don't know if she was with the dude but if you say she was then I believe you. All I know is after we heard about you, we ran to check on her and bring her to you and bro, she was fucked up."

"What you mean?"

"Blood was everywhere and she looked dead."

"Who the fuck did it? Everyone knows she can't fight." I was still pacing my room.

"The video was tampered with, therefore; we have no idea." I stopped and stared at him.

"Tell me you're lying."

"He ain't lying and why yo punk ass listen to him talk and not me?" Lil Faz came in talking shit like always. I ignored him and told them why I didn't wanna hear shit.

"Before Kim stabbed me, she showed me a video of C'Yani riding some dude. I figured it's her ex because we all know she's not that kind of woman."

"C is in love with you Meek. Are you positive it was her?"

"I wish I could say it was someone else but she was in the hotel room. All the bags I left were on the floor and from behind it was her hair and body shape. I didn't have to see her face to know it's her."

"Damn she doing it like that?" Lil Faz couldn't believe what I said either.

"Yup. Mind you I just fucked her before she went there. Can you believe she had him there?" The two of them looked at each other.

"Actually no." Shak said and I stared at him hop of my dresser.

"Think about it. She's scared of her own shadow so do you think she'd allow anyone to come in and record her?"

"Faz is right Meek. Why would she invite him there knowing you'd show up? Something ain't right about this entire situation." Now Shak began pacing.

"Let me ask C'Yani if she knows." I went to grab my keys and the two of them busted out laughing.

"What?"

"Nigga, she don't wanna see you."

"How you figure?"

"Well after Teri left the hospital and stopped stalking me for his ass." Lil Faz pointed to Shak who waved him off.

After Teri broke up with him, she's been contacting everyone in the family to get him to speak to her. Zia and Ty finally told her to stop calling them and if she really wanted Shakim, to go after him. She hasn't done it yet. I think she's scared because she doesn't know how he'll react. If you ask me, he'll probably be happy because he ain't been right ever since.

"He and I went in the room and only one of her eyes were open. She could barely speak, yet; asked for you." I felt like shit for not being there and hearing she asked for me didn't make it any better.

77

"Long story short, we didn't say anything. Her mom went to see her the next day, and come to find out she told her what you said. By the time we arrived she was checking out. She said to tell you and I quote, "*I never thought Meek would leave me to fend for myself. When you see him, tell him I don't ever want to see him again. My heart is broken and I'll never forgive him.*" I didn't say a word and couldn't help but think about Shak's comments. We had to figure out who did this to her and why. Meanwhile, I'm gonna get Kim and the first person to start with is her sister.

After leaving the hotel that night, Jasmine met me back at my house and I couldn't help but stare. She's definitely a gorgeous woman but her appearance seemed different. I didn't pay attention in the room because she basically attacked me at the door for sex. Unfortunately, I released early and that's because the two of us haven't really seen one another because she was hell bent on finding ways to hurt my ex.

I messed up with C'Yani and seeing her happy with another man bothers the hell out of me. However; it's not going to send me on a suicide mission trying to hurt her. The thug she's with now appears to be in love with her and I can't blame him because she's easy to love. I'm telling you if her sex would've been better, I wouldn't have gone elsewhere. It's not an excuse because I could have left but like all men, I was selfish.

Now here I am sleeping with her sisters' best friend who has some great pussy but everything else I could do without. The whining when she doesn't get her way. The attitudes over dumb shit and the hateful way she is towards my ex. To this day, I can't even tell you why she hates her. Women stay in competition but Jasmine be over doing it.

"Hey honey." I stood and kissed my mom on the cheek.

"Hey." She gave the waitress her drink order and placed her hands under her chin. Once she began to stare I knew some sort of lecture was coming on.

"How are you son?"

"Fine. Say what you need to." I glanced over the menu in front of me.

"Don't get sassy with me young man."

"You didn't ask me to meet you here for nothing. I know you have a few things on your mind." She grinned and placed her hand on the drink the waitress brought.

"If you insist." She gave me a fake smile, took a sip and glanced around the restaurant.

"When's the last time you went to the cemetery?" I sucked my teeth. I've gone maybe twice but didn't stay long. I don't know what to say at a gravesite and I never even saw or touched him. Granted it's my fault because I was with Jasmine but still. There was no connection so I don't know why, they kept asking me why.

"Tyrone, I know it's hard for you but think about how hard it is for C'Yani. She carried your son for nine months and pushed out a deceased child. She couldn't find you to bury him and whenever you see her, it's a non chalant attitude."

"Let me guess. You've been speaking to her?"

"I call and check on her once a week." I was aggravated because how she taking my mom calls and not mine?

"Ty are you sure about this new woman? I mean besides the sex is she better than C'Yani?" My mom backed away from the table a little as the waitress placed the appetizers in front of us. I ordered them before she arrived.

"Nah she's not." I thought about how perfect C'Yani was and I should've really spoken to her more in depth about how I was feeling.

"Ok then why didn't you sit C'Yani down and talk to her?" I shrugged my shoulders.

"Why the fuck did you ask her to marry you knowing your punk ass was fucking the other bitch?" We both looked

81

up at the thug and two of his friends. What the hell were they doing in an expensive place such as this? I peeked around him and no one seemed to be paying us any mind. Usually when big, thuggish men enter a facility, all eyes are on them but not here.

"Excuse us." My mom stood.

"Sit yo ass down. Ain't nobody talking to you." He used his hand to push her back in the chair by pressing down on her shoulder.

"Ty aren't you gonna day something?" I swallowed hard and stared up at them. I love my mother to death but we both know, I ain't no match for them.

"Yea Ty. Say something." Some dude with funny colored eyes taunted.

"Ma, this is the guy I spoke about who C'Yani is dealing with." Her eyes got big.

"Exactly!" I was about to ask them why they were at our table when my entire body was lifted out the seat and thrown against the window. I swear my back broke.

"Were you fucking C'Yani in a hotel?"

"What?" He placed a gun under my chin and I found myself holding in my urine. This is the second time he pulled one on me. When he did it at the house, I had just finished using the bathroom so the urge wasn't there but right now, I was terrified and my bladder was about to burst.

"You heard what the fuck I said."

"What we do is our business." He looked at the other guy and laughed.

"Your business huh."

"That's right, it is his business. Can someone contact the police please?" My mom screamed out and no one moved.

"The minute I stuck my dick in her, any business she has, is mine. I'm gonna ask you one more question and I expect an answer." I swallowed hard again and waited.

"Did you attack her in the hotel or do you know who did it?" I shook my head no back and forth.

"I'd never put my hands on her." He stared in my face and let me down. I started fixing my clothes.

"Ahhhhh." He punched me so hard in the stomach, it felt like my food from the past two days would come up. I felt a little urine slip out this time and I didn't care who noticed it. That shit hurt like hell.

"Please Stop." My mom cried out when he tossed me to the ground and kicked me a few times in the back and stomach.

"That's for cheating and leaving her to grieve for y'all son alone." He kneeled down and lifted my head. One of the guys had my mom by the hair.

"If she tells me you had anything to do with her attack, I'm going kill you and your stuck-up ass mother. Do I make myself clear?"

"Yes." I barely got out.

"Good." He banged my head into the ground and a tooth fell out. My vision was blurry but I could see my mom being tossed in a chair. Unfortunately, she fell and started screaming.

"Make sure these motherfuckers pay for their food." He barked and stared at me.

"You better leave a fucking tip too. My staff works hard." He winked and walked out. I've been here countless times and had no idea he owned it. How in the hell did we manage to dine in his restaurant?

"I think my ankle is broke." My mom cried out.

"Boss asked for us to escort you out." Two gentlemen towered over us.

"Can we get an ambulance?"

"Boss said take yourself to the hospital." The guy smirked.

"Do you want to pay with cash or credit?" He handed me the black card holder thing and I passed him my credit card. I didn't even bother looking at the price or seeing what they charged me for. All I know is, I couldn't take the chance of him not being told the food wasn't paid for. I used the chair to help myself up and put my hand out for my mom.

"Please tell me you didn't attack C'Yani." The guy handed me my card and I gave him a tip because I was too scared not to.

"Honestly, I have no clue what he's talking about." I opened the door and helped her as she limped out. Her foot is swollen so we both went to get checked out in the ER.

85

Whatever C'Yani has going on in her life doesn't have anything to do with me. But if she was attacked, I wonder if Jasmine is behind it. I'm gonna find out because I refuse to let this man and his thugs beat me up every time we see one another.

I'm no thug or fighter and I've never claimed to be. I tried to be down a few times but it wasn't for me. Anyway, I'm gonna have to see my ex and ask her to make him stop. This is beyond ridiculous. If I didn't know any better I'd say she has him strung out but that can't be possible because she's a dead lay; or is she?

"Honey are you sure about staying in the new house?"
My mom asked for the third time.

Ever since the attack, I've been staying with them. It's not that there's a problem, I just wanted to stay in the new condo I purchased. It wasn't far from them and all I could get last minute.

The house I've been looking at had a few potential buyers and the owners were still deciding who they wanted to sell it to. That's the only thing about buying from the owners themselves. They pick and choose who gets it, where if you go through agencies it doesn't matter. It's usually first come, first serve.

I loved the place too. It had four bedrooms, a huge kitchen which is good for me because I love to cook. There was a dining room, living room, family room and a full bathroom downstairs. Five bedrooms upstairs with a master bathroom and two others in the hallway. The attic and basement were finished so if I wanted to use that space for other stuff I could.

The best part is the house was only three years old. It still looked brand new and I guess it would be being they're only here in the summer. The woman had it built from the ground up and decided she wanted to move down to Florida, permanently.

I still don't speak to my sister and don't plan on it. She showed me her true colors when Jasmine came before me. I appreciated her visiting me in the hospital but it doesn't make me forget the reason for us not speaking. I'm not holding any grudges and honestly all I want is peace. However; I know just like she does with her friend working there, it won't be any.

I had no problem with Jasmine and still had no idea why the sudden change she had towards me. We used to hang out in the house of course because I didn't go anywhere but it was fun. She'd stay over my sisters sometimes with us if we had a girl's night and we never even thought to have any arguments. Out of nowhere, she became distant and started throwing shade as they say and the hatred towards me, showed more and more. One day, I asked what was the problem and she said, it wasn't one so I don't know. I washed my hands with it. I do know her working in the building isn't going to work out.

"I'm sure mom. No one knows about the place and I wanna keep it that way." I gave her a look.

"I'm not going to tell her C. I understand the situation better now and you're right about Teri hiring someone who doesn't like you." One thing I can say about my parents is they've always been fair.

"Thanks mom. I do need you to help me at the store. You feel like riding to Target?" My arm is still in a cast and I'd need help picking things up and putting them in the trunk and house. I needed comforters, dishes and other stuff to make me comfortable until the woman called me about the house. My furniture and clothes are there but the day I planned on shopping for the rest, I ran into Meek and got attacked.

"Sure, let me grab my things." I told her I'd meet her at the car. I opened the front door and froze. Why was he here?

"C'Yani let me talk to you." I tried to storm past him but my body was in pain from the bruised ribs so I was moving slow.

89

"I heard what happened and tried to see you at the hospital but the thugs security wouldn't let me in."

"Thugs?"

"You know the ones who came to my house with your boyfriend."

"They're not thugs Ty." They were but I also knew the other side of Meek and refused to call him that.

"C'Yani you know that guy barged in on me and my mom at the restaurant and blamed me for attacking you."

"Really?" I was shocked because after Meek left me in the hospital, I thought he didn't care.

"Why does he think I attacked you or know the person who did?" I gave him a weird look.

"I have no idea. Do you know who attacked me?"

"How could I C'Yani? I wasn't even there, nor do I have a clue on what he's talking about."

"Are you sure it was Meek?" I asked again because it's hard to believe he'd try to find out anything after the way he left me.

"I'm positive."

90

"Oh."

"He slammed me against the wall, punched me in the stomach and kicked me over and over."

"You're lying." I covered my mouth.

"You mean to tell me he didn't tell you?"

"No. I haven't spoken to him either. Why are you even here when you have a woman?"

"I don't have a woman and regardless I still love you." I laughed and opened my car door.

"Love would've never made you miss out on your son's birth."

"When are you gonna move on from that?" I walked up on him.

"Never Ty and you know why? Because he may not be here but he's still my son and his death is not something I could ever move on from." I turned to go back to my car because my mom was ready.

"Each day I try and forgive you but then I see you and your mouth spits out massive diarrhea. It shows me even though you may care a little, you still have no respect for the deceased. I hate you." I sat in the car and sped out the driveway. My mom had me pull over to switch spots. She said I'm driving reckless and I'm not about to kill her.

****

"Stay away from me." I shouted at Meek who was walking in my direction. Is it bother C'Yani day or something? First Ty and now him. My mom and I were placing the bags in the truck. How did he even know I was here?

"I'm going to run in Panera Bread. You want anything?" I looked at her because she never mentioned wanting food the entire time we been here.

"Ma. I want to go. We can grab something on the way."

"I'll only be a minute." She smiled at him and it was at that moment I realized she told him where we were. I noticed her on the phone in the store but paid it no mind.

"C'Yani can we talk?"

"No. When I wanted or should I say needed you, you left me hanging." I slammed the trunk down and walked to the driver's side of the door.

"Did you fuck Ty in the hotel room?" My mouth hit the floor.

"How dare you accuse me of being a whore?" I folded my arms across my chest the best I could with this cast.

"A whore?"

"Yes a whore. I slept with you before going to the room and here you are asking if I slept with my ex. A man I can't even stomach being around. A man who doesn't even care about the son we lost. A man who cheated on me because I couldn't please him in the bedroom. Do you think that low of me?"

"C, someone showed me a video of you riding a guy. I assumed it was him. It was the same hotel room, the bags I purchased you were on the floor and..."

"And what? It had to be me right because it's something I would do."

"C give me the benefit of the doubt." I chuckled.

"The benefit of the doubt is something you should've given me. Meek, I was in love with you and you shitted on me."

93

"Shitted on you?" He chuckled like always when I spoke differently. It didn't bother me because I'm used to it. I have to admit it does sound funny when I say it though.

"I was attacked by two people and they hurt me bad. Instead of you finding out the truth, you ran with what you assumed and left me. Left the woman you claimed to love and did me the same as him."

"I'd never do what he did. Don't compare me to that nigga."

"Oh no. So it wasn't you with some woman at the hotel a few nights ago." He ran his hand down his face.

"I saw you at the 7-11 and pulled in. I missed you so much and wanted to talk to you. Imagine my surprise when a woman stepped out behind you. Now I'm thinking you were being a gentleman and held the door for her being she got in her own vehicle. Funny how you sped out the parking lot and so did she. Me, being clueless as you call me followed thinking you were going home."

94

"C." He reached out for me and I snatched away. As much as I loved the way he held and touched me, I didn't want his hands anywhere near me.

"The minute you parked and took her hand in yours, I was crushed. You held it like she was your woman too. My heart broke in a million pieces because I needed you and just like him, you went elsewhere." Tears were racing down my face and my body started to shake.

"You were my man Meek. Mine! And just like that, another woman felt the pleasure you promised to never give away. How could you do me like that?" I started punching him in the chest. He didn't bother stopping me or even threaten me to do so. People were walking by staring.

"I didn't know and the video looked like you." He never even bothered denying it. I guess once I described in detail what I saw, he couldn't.

"And you wanted revenge. You had to hurt me the way I hurt you, right?" I wiped some of the tears falling.

"The only difference is, I could and would never want you to feel what I'm feeling right now." He tried to hug me and I pushed him off.

"I may be corny, stuck up, weird and whatever else you called me but I loved you Meek. I'm still in love with you but nothing you can say to me will make me forgive you. I hate you so much right now." It's like those words triggered something in him because he tossed me against the car.

"You can be mad all you want but I'm still your man." He forced a kiss on my lips and I smacked the hell out of him. His demeanor became even more angrier. I was definitely scared, yet; still said what I had to.

"How dare you kiss me with those same lips you kissed her with? Touching me with the hands you caressed her body with."

"Fuck! I'm sorry C." His hands were on top of his head as he paced back and forth in front of me.

"Now you're sorry. Were you sorry when you put your dick in her? Were you sorry for leaving me beat up in the hospital? Are you sorry for breaking my heart, even though you promised never to do it?"

"FUCKKKKKK!" He shouted again and punched the side of his truck leaving a dent. *What kind of strength does he have?* I backed away and opened the car door.

"Is everything ok?" My mom returned with a bag of food.

"Fine. I'm ready to go." She got in the car and closed the door.

"C'Yani." He grabbed my arm.

"Don't touch me. Don't you ever touch me again." I swatted his hands away and sat in the car.

"You don't mean that." I closed the door, locked it and cracked the window.

"I wish I didn't Meek. Stay out of my life and I'll stay out of yours." He tried to open the door but it was locked.

"You wanted freedom so have at it."

"C'YANI!" He shouted and I begged my mom to pull off. It took her a minute because he was banging on the window. I saw him in the side mirror jump in his truck and

97

speed out the parking lot. Oh well. He did this and I'm not going to feel bad for leaving him.

"Are you ok?"

"No but I will be." Even though we were in the car, I pulled my knees to my chest and cried like a baby. Another man I put my all in to cheated on me for what I assume is better. Maybe love isn't what I need to be dealing with. I asked God not to send any more men in my life. I'm not sure I can handle another heartache.

I watched C'Yani's mom pull off with her and stood there thinking about going after them. I knew if I did it wouldn't erase the pain and hurt I caused. Yea, I slept with the same chick I've been with since before her. I was horny and she wasn't speaking to me so I hit shorty up and like always, she was down.

The only reason she caught us at the store is because we both stopped there for condoms unbeknownst to the other. She followed me from there but I had no idea C saw us. Not like I wanted her to but it fucked me up to know she did. I made no plans of ever telling her if the truth came out about the shit with her ex. Especially, if we picked up where we left off but she caught me.

Tasty I been fucking her for a while. She used to be a stripper but claims to have a better job now, as if that would make me choose her to be my woman. *NOT!* We are strictly fuck buddies and that's it. Once I made C my woman I sent her a text telling her we were done. She knew what time it was and had no problem abiding by it. Shit, I've seen her out various times with C and she didn't even part her lips to acknowledge me.

She is definitely a woman who knew her position. That's why when I hit her up she made sure to ask if I were in a relationship. In my head, C'Yani slept with that nigga so I told her no. I should've waited and found out the truth but it was too late.

It's funny how she spoke of me accusing her to be a whore. I don't even know why I let Kim get in my head with the video. Now that I think of it, she probably set it up and had someone attack C. I couldn't wait to find the bitch and had tons of people looking out for her.

The only thing fucking with me today is watching C'Yani cry. My heart was breaking and I felt like shit. She's right about us not breaking up, therefore; I was still her man. I didn't look at it the way she did but from her point of view I messed up. I knew better and risked everything with her for pussy I could've held out on.

Ever since I been with C, fucking shorty didn't even feel the same. Her moaning and sucking me off was good and all but I wanted it to be C. I ended up sleeping with her once that night and bouncing. Right then I knew C'Yani still had my heart and I had to see her.

****

"How's it going Pops?" He's been out the hospital for two days and stayed with my grandparents. None of us wanted him to go home because we had no idea where Kim was.

"Better."

"You look better." He nodded.

"How's C'Yani?" I plopped down on the chair next to him.

"I did what you told me and made her talk to me. The thing is, she knows everything." He shook his head. I told him about her ignoring my calls and messages.

After Shak told me what happened, I wanted to see her but she refused. I contacted her mom and it just so happened they were in target so I raced over thinking she had to speak. Oh, she spoke alright and said a lotta things that made me realize I am the same nigga who did her dirty. I was her man

101

and cheated when she needed me. The situations were different but the rest is the same.

"What are you gonna do?"

"Nothing I can do. She doesn't wanna see me and smacked fire from my ass when I kissed her."

"What? And she's still alive?" He started laughing. He knows I don't play that woman hitting a man shit.

"I know right."

"You must really be in love to let her get away with it." I had my elbows on my knees staring at the wall.

"I am but I fucked up. I promised never to do those things and did them anyway. I'm no better than him."

"I don't think she's done with you." He had a slight grin in his face.

"You had to see her. Nothing on her face said she'll give me another chance."

"Good for your ass." My grandmother walked in talking shit as usual.

"When we tried to tell you what happened, you acted like a got damn baby. Had you listened she'd still be around.

102

Now I gotta go see her to bring food and play cards." Me and my pops stared at her.

"What?"

"When did you playing cards start?"

"If you must know, a week before she was attacked. All of y'all were out doing who knows what and she came over to see Ty and Zia who were up visiting. You two weren't speaking so it was no need to mention it." I found it funny how my grandmother seemed to like her and now were no longer together.

"I'm gonna say this Meeky and leave it alone." She handed my dad his pain pills. I don't bother to take mine because even though the pain is bad sometimes, I hate the groggy feeling.

"C'Yani isn't your normal video vixen or the type of woman who's gonna fight over you."

"I know."

"I'm serious Meek. We all know she's not a fighter but even if she were, her mentality is different. Shit, she didn't even fight for the no good nigga before you and they had five years." I looked up at her.

"Yea we talk a lot. I know all about you turning her out too but we not talking about that." My pops turned to me and I busted out laughing.

"She was a virgin?"

"Nah but she may as well be. Dude before me didn't show her shit." He shook his head and my grandmother sucked her teeth.

"Anyway, she really loved you Meek and all of us think she's the best woman for you. However; like most men you thought with your dick and let the pride get in the way and lost her."

"Yea but you can talk to her for me."

"HELL NO! Do you know she made us some lasagna and I had to ask for the recipe? I have never tasted food that good besides my own."

"What does her cooking have to do with this?"

"Duh! How am I going to get her to cook for me with yo ass tryna make me have her talk to you. Your ass better think of something."

"I don't like to agree with my mom a lot but..."

WHAP! My grandmother popped him on the head.

"She's right son. You hurt her the same way her ex did and it's gonna take a lot of begging and pleading to win her back." I fell back on the sofa tryna come up with ways. I stared at my grandmother, stood and went to the door.

"I'm gonna tell her you're hurt and wanna see her."

"Boy, you better not." I smiled and ran out.

"Yes I am. Love you though." I blew her a kiss and went to my car. My phone began vibrating and when I looked it was Tasty asking me to stop by her crib. I told her to text me the address because as long as we messed around, we only meet up at the hotel.

I ain't have shit to do so I drove over and blew the horn for her. She came out and I had to adjust myself. The clothes were tight and regardless of the way we departed the last time, she still turned me on.

"Hey." She hopped in my truck. *First mistake.* The only woman who's been in here is C because it's brand new. And dumb ass Kim who I tossed out on the highway.

"You good?" She started fiddling with my jeans and pulled my dick out. *Second mistake.* Never let a chick who ain't your woman give you head in yo shit. You never know who'll drive by.

"What you doing? Shittttt." I didn't even fight because once her lips wrapped around me it was over.

I used my hand to guide her head up and down. The way she gobbled my man up had me thinking about taking her in the house. She started making the sucking noises and jerked me faster. Just as I was about to cum, I opened my eyes and C'Yani was coming in my direction. *What the hell is she doing over here?* She stopped next to my truck and smiled. Here I thought she was mad and she stopped to speak. Tasty must've heard her ask if we could talk because she went faster. I tried my hardest to stop her but it was no use.

"Fuckkkk! Got dammit." I all but shouted and C looked at me.

106

"Are you ok?" She appeared to be concerned and I felt like shit.

"Yea he's fine." Shorty popped up wiping her mouth and smiled.

"Oh... umm... I didn't mean to interrupt."

"Shit." I jumped out the truck like an idiot and my jeans were still open. My dick was hanging out and the look on C'Yani's face said it all.

"Why did I even think about giving you another chance?" She glanced at shorty in the truck and shook her head.

"C wait!" I reached out but she sped off.

"Fuck that stuck up bitch." I spun around fast.

"Tha fuck you just say?"

"You don't want her stuck up ass. She can't do shit for you."

"Get out!" I zipped up my jeans.

"Why you mad at me?" She had her arms folded.

"Why you call me over here?" I went to the other side and pulled her out the truck because she wouldn't move. What is it about women not getting out when you tell them to?

"Because the last time wasn't the same and I wanted some more."

"We're done." I slammed the door and started walking to the other side.

"What?"

"You heard me. We're finished. Don't hit my line again." I opened my door and turned to see her pouting.

"Yo. How do you even know her?" I was curious because she called her stuck up. She had to know her in order to say it.

"She's my boss." I fell against the truck and blew my breath. What are the fucking odds? I hopped in my truck and drove home knowing I fucked up again with C.

"Your sister still not speaking to you?" Jasmine asked while we sat in VIP at Shakim's club. I missed C'Yani and even though I went to the hospital every day when she was hurt, she still had no words for me. I'm not saying she hates me but when she doesn't wanna speak, she won't.

"No. I don't blame her. I should've spoken to her about hiring you." She sucked her teeth. I didn't think it would be a problem with her working there. Yes, they don't fuck with each other like that but I had no idea it would be an issue with her opening an office.

"Don't get mad. It's the same as if you had a building and I let her run an office out of it. We all know y'all don't really fuck with each other." She waved her hand.

"That's your sister who don't like me." I looked at her. She may not come out and say it but anyone on the outside looking in can tell Jasmine is jealous of C. No idea why when she's just as pretty but women these days are always in competition for nothing.

109

Jealousy is one thing but around me, Jasmine doesn't talk bad shit about my sister so I don't know why everyone jumped down my throat. Unless she's doing shit I don't see and if that's the case, trust I will address it.

"Have you ladies decided on what to drink?" The waitress asked.

"I'll have a red wine and water." Jasmine stared at me. No one besides my parents knew about my pregnancy and I planned on keeping it that way until Shakim knows.

Ever since he left the hospital, I haven't been able to reach him. Lil Faz finally told me to stop calling him or he's gonna break my phone and crash my new car. I swear they have to be the rudest family I've ever met. Even Mystic who isn't in the streets as much, has the same amount of ignorance. I blame big Fazza though. That man is wayyyyyyy past aggressive and rude. The only person he listens to is his mom, his daughters who are spoiled by him and his wife. She is the only one to really shut him down though and I get a kick out of it everytime.

As far as my new car, I purchased a 2018 Infinity. It's nothing like my Tesla but it's safe and not electric. The insurance company told me there were some electrical issues, which is why the door wouldn't open and they're still unsure about why it filled with gas. They can tell me whatever but I know for a fact, Barb had something to do with it. I'm waiting on the full report from the Tesla people to come in.

"I'll have a shot of Tito's and a Malibu Bay Breeze." The waitress walked away and Jasmine grilled me.

"Is there something you wanna tell me?" I picked my phone up and checked for the tenth time to see if Shak even looked at my message. We both had the iPhone so when it turned blue it meant he unblocked me. But nope. Still green. I can't believe he's that mad because of a choice I made to stay safe.

"Not at all. You know I'm here to see Shakim and if I'm drunk, I'll probably miss him."

"Oh ok. I was about to say."

"Say what heffa?"

"I was about to say…" She was cut off in the middle of her sentence.

"What the fuck you doing here Teri?" Shak stood there with Meek, who had his face turned up staring at Jasmine. Why don't these men like her? Did she do something to them I don't know about?

"It's a free country and last time I checked, this club is for anyone. Right Jas?"

"Bitch. Don't open your mouth." Meek barked.

"Don't worry Meek. I won't say a word about..." he snatched her up by the hair and tossed her to the floor. Security came in and removed her from the area.

"Go home Teri."

"No and I don't appreciate you and your cousin harassing my friend." He smirked.

"You have no fucking idea who she is and stay defending her." The waitress walked in with our drinks.

"She's not staying." He stopped her from passing it to me.

"You're being ridiculous."

112

"Say what you want but you're not staying." I rolled my eyes and stood up.

"FINE!" I stormed past him, pushing his shoulder and went down the steps. I came to talk and here he is being an ass.

"What up sexy?" Some guy grabbed my hand and I smiled. He was sexy and had I not still been in love with Shak, he could get it.

"Hey." I saw Shak staring at me from upstairs and waved.

"You got a man?"

"Nope."

"Good because I wouldn't let you out my sight if you were my woman." He licked his lips.

"Move on Teri." Shak pushed me towards the door.

"Yo my man." The dude stood.

"You don't want these problems." Meek said and I rolled my eyes at both of them.

"Keep walking."

"Shak baby. When are you coming back to our section?" I stopped and turned around. The bitch was fucking gorgeous and rubbing up and down his chest with a smile on her face.

"Y'all section?"

"Umm yea our section. It's the same one we had for the past three weeks. You wanna join us?" The woman said without a care in the world.

"Oh really. Ok then." I walked outside, grabbed Jasmine who was mad as hell, walked back in and dared him to touch me or her. No idea where the chick went but Shak was right in my face.

"YO! You think I'm playing with you?" He snatched my arm and swung me around.

"Frankly I don't give two shits about what you do from this point on. Continue doing you and stop blocking me from fucking." I could tell me mentioning sleeping with another man had him pissed.

"I wish you would get mad when you got her a section. Like really? You doing it like that?" I pointed to the VIP are where his cousins were surrounded by tons of women and a few other dudes.

"Teri."

"Don't fucking Teri me." I was face to face with him now.

"I thought coming here to speak and share some good news with you would bring us together again but you're still the same nigga. The same nigga who can't keep his dick from in between a bitches' legs because him and his girl are going through something." He tried to grab my arm and I snatched it away.

"I broke up with you because I was scared of what happened. It was unfair to you and I've tried to apologize over and over but you blocked me and had your family tell me not to contact them. I get it but I thought after seeing one another you'd realize the same as I, and that's, that we're meant to be. The fucking joke is on me tho. Enjoy your night." I walked off with Jasmine behind me. I assumed he would come after me but nope.

"You ok?" She asked on the way to the bathroom.

"Yea. Let me wipe my face and we can go." I opened the door and two women were standing there talking. I paid them no mind until one mentioned Shak by name.

"Yea girl. I heard he's working with something and he can go all night if you let him."

"I thought he had a chick and was off the market." The other one leaned in and applied lip gloss.

"That's what they say but she must not have kept him happy because he sure been slinging his dick everywhere." I turned the water on and splashed some on my face.

"If that's the case, I'm damn sure about to try and ride his ride." Both women slapped hands and walked out.

I held in the new tears tryna fall, fixed my face and stepped out the bathroom only to run into the same two women standing in front of Shak. Some other chick stood by Meek with her arms folded. I guess my sister wasn't messing with him either.

Shak and I locked eyes. I rolled mine, gave him the finger and headed to the door. A different guy approached me. He was handsome, dressed nice and had a couple of guys with

116

him. His face was familiar but by the time I realized who he was, gunfire broke out in the club.

People were screaming and running everywhere to get out the way. Jasmine pulled me down and we crawled behind the bar. When the shooting stopped we sat there. The bartenders and other people were with us but no one said a word until we heard the cops yelling.

"Shit. That's crazy." I stood wiping my clothes and made sure I had my stuff.

"Ummm. Teri." Jasmine pointed and Shak was cradling someone in his arms. We made our way over and Meek laid there with blood pouring out but I had no clue from where. The paramedics rushed in and left just as fast with Shak behind them.

"I have to call his family." I pulled my phone out and dialed lil Faz.

"What Teri? That nigga said if I told him you called again he's gonna shoot me. Ain't nobody got time to be dying over you." I wanted to laugh but caught myself.

"Faz, Meek was shot at the club and..." I heard a noise and looked down to see the phone disconnected. I tried to call back but he didn't answer.

"What happened?"

"He hung up." I shrugged my shoulders and walked to my car.

"I see you didn't die." Barb had a grin on her face. All she did was confirm she had something to do with what happened to me.

Jasmine looked at me with a smirk and in two seconds flat we were beating the brakes off this bitch. Slamming her head in the ground, stomping her and anything else we could. I felt someone lift me off, toss me against the car and began reading me my rights. Just my luck I get arrested for this bitch. Maybe it's best I stay away from Shak because clearly, she's not.

"Come on Meek. Don't die on me." I watched as the paramedics worked on him in the back of the ambulance.

I don't even know how he got hit. One minute I'm watching Teri leave and this punk stops her and the next, they start shooting. I could tell by Teri's reaction she figured out who he was when it became too late. All the talks we had, she knew like we all did those niggas would return. Unfortunately, with everything going on I put them on the back burner to deal with other shit. Looks like I shouldn't have because my damn cousin got hit.

The minute we realized who they were, both of us started shooting. The only question is how did they walk in with guns? There's a strict policy about entering with any sort of weapons. It's obvious they knew someone because security at the door is tight and knows we don't play that shit.

"Let's go." The back door opened at the hospital and they all jumped out.

"You gonna be good cuz. I'll be right here." His eyes were closed but I prayed he heard me. I hopped out and was about to make a call when lil Faz came running over and hugged me.

"How the hell did you find out? I was just about to call everybody."

"You're stalking ass girlfriend." That's when I remembered Teri being in the club. It's funny how they still called her my girlfriend even though we haven't spoken.

"Shit. Is she alright?" We may not be a couple but I still loved her and would never wish harm on her.

"I don't know man. I heard Meek was shot, hung up and raced over here. Everyone is on the way." I nodded and picked my phone up to make sure Teri didn't get hit, when a police car pulled up with a chick in the back. He stepped out, went in, returned with a nurse and wheelchair and opened the door.

"Is that?-" Lil Faz had to hold me back from going after Barb. This is the first time I'm seeing her since the accident with Teri. Her hair was messed up, clothes torn, one shoe missing and blood poured from her mouth and nose. We started laughing, which made her look in our direction.

"Tell your bitch it's on next time I see her."

"My bitch." I was confused because none of those ho's I'm sleeping with are my main.

"Teri. Her and that bitch jumped me but I got something for her. She better stay in jail."

"Jail?"

"Yup and I'm pressing charges." I tried to kill that bitch. Security and two other cops had to hold me back.

"Calm down sir before we arrest you too." I broke free and walked off. I called Teri's phone to see if she were lying but no one answered. Once I called the police station and they confirmed her being there, it only pissed me off more.

I stormed in the hospital only to see the cops standing outside Barb's door. It's no way I can get to her but I made sure to walk by and let her know, I'm gonna kill her. I didn't use any words and once our eyes connected she stared down at my hand that was touching my waist. Her eyes grew and she knew then, I'm coming for her. I smiled knowing she got the point and ran into my aunt and uncle who looked disheveled.

"Is he ok?" They asked at the same time.

"They took him in the back. We have to wait now." We all took a seat in the waiting room for what felt like hours. I heard a pair of heels and all of us looked up to see C'Yani. Shocked is an understatement because none of us expected to see her. Meek explained how she caught him getting his dick sucked and her speeding off. I guess when you hear of a loved one being shot all that other shit goes out the window.

"How is he?" She went straight to my aunt who embraced her. My uncle tried and she pushed him off.

"We're still waiting to hear. How did you find out?"

"Teri called my mom from jail." She gave me a hard stare.

"And told her Meek was shot."

"Why are you here though?" She had her hands on her hips looking at my cousin. He stayed fucking with her.

"Lil Faz don't start with me."

"I'm just saying." He started laughing.

"I don't want him to die fool. Do you mind if I wait with you?" We all looked at her.

"Sit yo white ass down with the rest of us." Big Faz walked in and so did everyone else. As usual it was a comedy show in the waiting room. Three hours later the doctor walked out and took a seat next to us.

"Mr. Gibson suffered a gunshot to his abdomen and leg. The one in his leg was the hardest to remove because it was stuck in between the muscle. The one in his abdomen did some damage as well with his intestines but we were able to fix him right up. He's asleep now and will be placed in a room after leaving recovery. Does anyone have questions?"

"Will he be able to run after our little one?" All of us turned around and the bitch Theresa, Tasty, whatever her name is, he got caught with was rubbing her stomach. I thought C'Yani was gonna throw up by the amount of gagging she did.

"Yea. I just found out we're expecting." None of us said a word as we all stared at C.

"He should be fine in a few months or even weeks depending on his recovery time. Anything else?"

"No thank you." My uncle said and shook his hand. He's still recovering himself from the shit Kim's crazy ass did.

"Who the fuck are you?" Zia stood in her face. Meek is her favorite and the only person he introduced the family to is C'Yani, so she's probably wondering like the rest of us. If this bitch is pregnant though he can forget C ever taking him back.

"I'm Theresa and we've been together for a year and a half."

"A year and a half. That's funny because this woman right here, is the only one we know of." She pointed to C.

"Oh, I know all about her. She's the chick he cheated on with me. I'm not sure why she's even here when we were just having sex outside my house in his truck. Ain't that right?" She looked over at C and so did we. I know about the dick sucking but not the other shit.

"I'm gonna go. Thankfully, he's gonna be ok." Just like C'Yani not to involve herself in drama. It's one of the things my cousin loves about her.

"You ain't gotta go C but this ho does." Ty rose to her feet.

"Ho?"

124

"Damn right. If you knew he had a woman why did you sleep with him?"

"I had him first and you're questioning me, when you should be asking him. I didn't make him sleep with me."

"Have a good day everyone." C'Yani walked out and I ran behind her.

"C stop." I turned her body around and tears were falling down her face.

"The sad part about this is, I can't even get mad because we aren't together. But why did he make a baby with her?" I hugged her until she calmed down.

"C, wait until he wakes up and find out if it's true. Meek told me you're her boss so she may be saying it to be spiteful." She stared up at me.

"Why would she do that?"

"You have no idea the things women will do for a man's attention."

"I guess."

"Go home and I'll make sure my aunt contacts you when his eyes open." She nodded and wiped her face. I knew she still loved Meek and the same goes for him.

"Are you leaving?"

"Yes. I have to stop by the club to survey the damage and then check on your sister."

"Oh ok. Talk to you later." I walked her to the car, sent a text to my cousins and went to my first destination. After staying for two hours, I went straight to Teri's. Her car was in the driveway and all the lights were off. I used my key and was shocked to see it still worked.

I locked up, went in one of the guest's rooms to shower and tossed my clothes in the trash. Meeks blood covered them so it's no need to keep any of it. I stepped in Teri's room and watched her sleep for a few minutes. I missed the hell outta her. I sat on the bed gently, moved the strands of hair out her face and kissed her lips.

"I'm pregnant." She whispered and rolled over. *Say What?*

126

"What the fuck you say?" He forced my body to turn towards him.

"If you don't want it, I'll be fine raising the baby on my own."

"Slow the hell down. Is it mine?" I gave him an evil look.

"I don't know how far along you are."

"You should've asked before assuming I share my pussy, the way you share your dick." I tossed the covers off, went in the bathroom and slammed the door. I didn't have to go because I just got out the shower maybe ten minutes before he arrived. I had dosed off until his lips touched mine. It didn't make me nervous at all that he crept in. He's the only one with a key besides my family.

"How far are you?" I never heard him open the bathroom door.

"Three months now." He smiled. I guess that's his way of knowing the baby is his. I moved past and went back to bed.

"When did you find out?"

127

"The day I almost died and don't you get mad for me not telling you." His face was tight.

"It's the reason I wanted to be away from you. I was scared of not only losing it with the crazy people in your life but I don't want the same thing to happen..." "He didn't let me finish.

"What happened to your sister isn't going to happen to you."

"I'm not even mother material Shak. I love to party and..."

"You'll be fine."

"But we're not a couple and I don't wanna be fighting chicks over you. My sister still isn't talking to me, I beat Barb's ass and got arrested. It's so much going on." He shushed me with his lips and I melted in his arms.

"You're stressing over nothing Teri. Let daddy relax you." He dropped his towel and as bad as I wanted to give him head, I held off. I remember those women discussing him sleeping with different chicks over the last few weeks. I reached in the nightstand, grabbed the box of condoms and handed them to him.

"The hell is this? You been fucking other niggas?"

"Hell no but you been sleeping with other chicks. Until you get tested again, I am notttttt." He shut me right up when he spread my legs and ran his tongue up and down. My body quivered and the desire I had for him increased.

"Cum in my mouth Teri." In five seconds flat, my juices squirted in his mouth. My nub continued pulsating and being the best pussy eating man, I've ever encountered, he made sure to have me release over and over. I couldn't help but scream out.

"I ain't wearing no got damn condoms and no bitch in this world has ever felt me raw. You're the only woman who will always get this." He entered and stretched my lower half. My nails were leaving indents in his biceps as he dug deeper.

"Shit T. No other woman has me wide open the way you do."

"I love you Shakim." He sat back and used his hands to hold him up as he watched me ride.

"I love you too T. No bitch out here can fuck with you even on your bad days." He bit down on his lip as I dropped harder feeling the base of his dick hit my pussy.

"Fuck your man T."

"You're my man."

"Yup and don't break up with me again." He forced his mouth on mine and thrusted into me from the bottom.

"Oh God. Shakimmmmmm. Baby, I can't..."

"Yes you can. Let that shit go." I nodded, kissed him and rode that wave to pleasure.

"Turn over." I collapsed on the bed until he lifted my lower half up, spread my legs and moved in and out slow. He knew this was my favorite position.

"Throw that ass back for me." Once he smacked it, I lost control and came again. He had a way of pushing me to my limits in the bedroom.

"I'm finna come T." I couldn't respond because my clit was so hard I'm bound to explode with him. I clenched the sheets, threw my ass back one good time and felt him digging in my cheeks.

"ARGHHHHH! SHITTTT!" He fell on the bed and pulled me next to him.

"That's the best sex I've had in a very long time." I pulled the covers up and laid on his chest.

"Me too." I felt the tears leaving my eyes and tried to wipe them.

"No need to shed tears T. I'm not going anywhere." He lifted my head and wiped them away.

"I'm sorry Shakim. I was scared." He moved my body on his.

"I was scared too Teri. It's my first time being in love but I never would've left you. If you do it again, baby or not I won't come back." I nodded.

"I'll still fuck you though because ain't no other man gonna feel this." He slid me down on his semi erect dick.

"I'm tired Shak. Oh shit." He now had me against the wall giving me the best dick down I ever received. With him it's always different and way past satisfying.

"I'm about to make love to you." He kissed my lips and laid me on the bed.

"Can you go longer?" I nodded my head yes even though my ass was tired as fuck. I'm glad I did because the two of us were moaning out for each other all night. I cried again when he mentioned all the times he wanted to call but his pride wouldn't let him. It only proved he missed me the same.

****

"I want you to move in with me." It was the next day and he woke up when his cousin called to say Meek is asking for him.

"Shak." I started the shower.

"Teri, I can't protect you here and I need that sexy body with my seed in her next to me every night."

"I don't know. I'm used to my independence."

"You want me to move here?" He turned his face up.

"Don't come for my house."

"I'm saying. Mine is much bigger but if you wanna stay here then I'll move my stuff in."

"Shakim are you sure? You still sleeping with other women."

"The minute our bodies became one last night, all those other bitches went on knock off. Teri, I'd never disrespect you like that."

"How did I get you to love me?" He stepped in the shower with me.

"Shit. I should be asking you that question."

"Under all your ignorance, Shakim you are a great man who loved me with all my flaws and ain't afraid to put me in my place. I love your arrogance and the way you make love to me and then turn around and fuck me. You've taken my body to new heights and I don't want anyone else touching me but you." He smiled.

"You ain't got to worry about that. Can't nobody substitute daddy." He leaned down to kiss me.

"I love you T and you're the only woman who could make me settle down. It's been a task all the women tried to accomplish for years and you did it in no time. It's the real reason they hate you."

"Too bad. I'm not letting you go anymore."

"Good because my dick ain't been satisfied until last night."

"You better not have fucked them raw." I squatted down to please him.

"Ssssss." He stared down at me. He knows I love for him to watch.

"I would've taken a test for you T. Got damn you do me good." I gave him what he waited for and stood.

"And so do you. It's good to know you would've done it." I kissed him and washed both of us up. We stepped out and I handed him a towel before going in the room to get some of his clothes out the drawer. I never took them out.

"Who the fuck banging on your door like that?" I shrugged and he went down the steps in his wife beater and sweats.

"The hell you want?" It had to be Jasmine if he talking like that.

"You and Meek are gonna stop coming at me. I don't do shit to y'all and I've been keeping his little secret under wraps."

"Don't nobody give a fuck about you bitch. The grimy shit you doing is gonna come out."

"What grimy shit and secret is she talking about?" I walked down the steps in my robe.

"Bitch tell her since you're so tough." Shakim stood in front of Jasmine with his arms folded. She said nothing.

"Exactly! Get your dumb ass the fuck up outta here."

"You talking all that shit but did you tell her the secret? Huh? You want me to tell her and you ain't said nothing either." Now it was her turn to cross her arms.

"Somebody better tell me something." The look he gave Jasmine made me nervous.

"We'll talk later about it." He ran up the steps to gather his things to see Meek.

"I'll call you in a few." He pecked my lips and looked her up and down.

"This hateful and jealous bitch is not coming over when you move in." He shoulder checked her so hard she fell against the wall. What type of secret has them hating each other?

"You're moving in with him?" I questioned Teri when Shak left.

"I haven't said yes but he did ask." She went up the steps and I waited for her in the living room. If she's moving in with him I won't be able to visit. It also means Barb is definitely on knock off. We've been working too hard to keep them apart. How the hell did they even end up together anyway?

I paced her living room tryna figure out ways to keep her from moving in and really couldn't find any. Word on the street is, when he claimed Teri no woman could get him to pay her any mind. If she moves in its gonna happen again, which means I won't get Meek to fuck me. I don't even want him anymore. Me sleeping with him is to hurt C'Yani.

Unfortunately, he was shot at the club and will need time to recuperate. I wonder if C'Yani is the woman he asks to help because when I was coming out my friend's house, I noticed some chick get in his truck. I don't know what happened but the bitch pulled next to him, turned her face up and sped off. He snatched the chick out the car and left too. What type of control did she have over Meek?

In the few years I've known him, he's never been smitten over a chick. He may have been with his ex but I wouldn't know because he was finished with her before we met.

"What's this secret?" She came down dressed in a fitted sweat suit and asked me to take a ride with her to the mall. I ain't have shit else to do plus it would give me time to ask questions.

"Well."

"Well what?" I text Ty from my phone to fuck. I was horny as hell thinking of Meek.

"The secret?" I waved her off.

"Girl ain't no secret." She gave me a weird look at the red light.

"It's not. That's why he tried to call me out. He knew I didn't have one. Anyway, what's this about you moving in?" I put my phone up when he text back ok.

"Nothing really. He stopped by late last night and we talked."

"Only talked?"

"We did more than talk and once he found out about the baby he..."

"Baby? Bitch, you let him get you pregnant?"

"Is it a problem?"

"Hell yea." She pulled in the mall parking lot.

"And why is that?"

"Teri you can do much better than this. You know he got hella ho's and a baby ain't gonna keep him." I stepped out and slammed the door.

I'm not even sure why it angered me this much. Maybe it's because he's not gonna allow her around me. No more free parties and vacations all over. Hell no, this will not be happening.

"Why the hell are you so mad? What I do with my man is none of your business."

"It is my business when he's controlling you."

"Controlling me?"

"Ugh yea. He already told you I can't come over when you move with him. He made you leave the club, well tried to anyway. It's clear he doesn't care for me. What's gonna happen when you have the baby? I can't see him or her? I don't know about you but he's tryna control you and that's not love."

"Are you serious right now?" She asked and I could see tell she was thinking about what I said, which is what I wanted.

"Yup."

"You know what? I'm gonna return you to your car because you're on some other shit." She turned the car back on.

"I'm on other shit? I'm not the one about to leave my friend in the cold for a nigga you only been with a few months."

"Let's just go."

"Nah I'm good. I wouldn't want your boyfriend to stop you from giving me a ride."

"What is it about Shak you don't like? You've never cared for him and to this day, I don't know why."

139

"Do you not remember he pulled a gun out on me the first night? Then, he verbally attacks me every time he sees me and you say nothing." She stood there not saying a word.

"Exactly. So don't ask me why I don't like him when he's been coming for me since day one." I walked off to go in the mall. Fuck her. Ty will pick me up.

"Don't call me when he cheats or his controlling ways turn into abusive ones." I stepped through the glass doors and watched as she left. If this goes as planned, she's gonna continue thinking about what I said and distance herself from him. Teri may he hood, ghetto and ratchet at times but she's gullible as hell to certain things; me being one of them. Oh well.

****

"Why you here without your car?" Ty asked after picking me up. He was at work so it took him a few hours to get me. I didn't mind because I still had his credit card and used it in every store I went in.

"Teri brought me. We were supposed to shop together but she got in her feelings."

140

"About?" He parked in front of his house and we stepped out.

"Her boyfriend wants her to move in with him."

"So what's the problem?" He used his key to open the door and locked it after I walked in.

"He doesn't like me, which means he most likely won't let me see her at his place."

"Who cares Jasmine? She can see you at your place. Why you make things more difficult than they have to be?"

"Whatever." I waved him off and started walking up the steps.

"Did you attack C'Yani at a hotel?" I froze and turned around.

"What?" He leaned against the door frame looking sexy as hell.

"Her man beat my ass in the restaurant because he said someone attacked her. Oh, and he asked if we fucked. The only person in the hotel room with me, is you." He came towards me.

"How did he know we were there?" I wrapped my arms around his neck and kissed him. I had to find a way to distract him from this conversation. Not because he'd be mad I didn't answer but because he had a way of knowing when I'm lying.

"Fuck Jasmine. Shit." I rushed to put his dick in my mouth and just like that we were fucking like rabbits.

After we finished, I laid in his arms and thought about different ways to get the bitch. It's obvious, I have to use other people now to keep the heat off me. The other thing is making sure Ty doesn't look into the situation. Whether he's with C'Yani or not, he still loves her and I could see how upset he'd be finding out something happened to her. I refuse to be the woman he leaned on over her. I'll be there for my man if need be but not for another bitch.

I stared at the ceiling in the hospital room listening to my family discuss some shit I knew nothing about. No one noticed me open my eyes yet and the conversation flowed as if I were part of it. What I couldn't understand is how those niggas stepped in the club with weapons and why this bitch saying she pregnant by me?

The worst part of that situation is hearing Ty and Zia describe how hurt C'Yani was. I didn't think she'd come after catching me getting my dick sucked but I'm glad she did, yet; in the midst of it all she's hurt again. Maybe it's best for me to leave her alone at this point.

She's a great woman; actually, perfect and I come into her life only to make it worse. I'm definitely in love with her and I can see us spending the rest of our lives together as a family but like my grandfather said, she's not about to let me walk all over her.

It's not as if I'm doing it on purpose. I thought she slept with her ex and instead of hearing her side, I dipped out. Then, she wanted to talk and ran into me in an uncompromising

143

position. And now this dumb bitch claiming to be pregnant. If that's not enough to make a woman leave, I don't know what is. I hate the fact I even placed myself in this situation.

"I didn't expect to hear from you." Tasty walked in the room and started removing her clothes.

"Why is that?" I sat on the sofa to take my sneakers off and looked up to see her fully exposed.

"You have a woman."

"Had. We aren't together anymore and you should know that if I'm here with you."

"Ok. I just thought you..." I cut her off.

"Nah shorty. My woman or should I say ex, has the best pussy I've ever had. There wasn't a need to cheat when everything I needed was in front of me. You only here now because I wanna fuck." I laid back on the couch and stared at her.

I had no business being here but it's been a minute since I got out the hospital and I was horny. C'Yani isn't taking my calls and I don't blame her. I left her in the hospital and until my cousin explained what happened, I didn't bother finding out the truth.

"Can you at least let me feel your tongue?" I busted out laughing. She's been tryna get me to eat her pussy for the longest. Mind you she used to be a stripper so why in the hell would I do it? I'm not calling her a ho, but shit we know what most of them do in the clubs.

"Never. You can suck my dick tho." I pushed her head down and enjoyed the sight before me. After I came, she laid back on the floor, gapped her legs open and started playing with herself. My dick began rising immediately.

"You like this baby?" I hated to hear her call me pet names. You only do that with your man and she knows damn well I ain't hers.

"Get the condoms." She stood and walked over to the table.

"Here." She handed them to me because I don't play that shit of the woman opening them.

"Hurry up Meek." She straddled my lap and grinded her wet pussy on me. My dumb ass fucked around and allowed

her to slide down as I opened the condom. It felt good but not
as good as C.

"Oh shit Meek. I never experienced you without a
wrapper. You feel so got damn good." She stood on her feet
and rode the shit outta me. C was on my mind the entire time.

"Yo, I'm about to cum." I lifted her up just in time and
came on myself.

"I gotta go." I stood, grabbed my things and hauled
ass outta there. I haven't seen her since.

How could I fuck her without a condom? Now she's
saying I got her pregnant. Unless some pre-cum slipped in her,
I'm not sure it's mine.

"Thank goodness you're awake." I heard her voice.

"GET THE FUCK OUT!" I barked and she jumped
back.

"Baby don't speak to me that way. Our child will feel
the stress and..." I sat up the best I could, wrapped my hand
around her throat and pulled her close. I swear stitches were
busting open because the pain became unbearable and it felt
like blood began to seep out.

146

"You in here lying to my family about a got damn baby. Then you said the shit in front of C'Yani to hurt her." I squeezed tighter.

"I doubt that's my kid but if you are pregnant and it is, I'm taking it because you're only keeping it for a check."

"Let go Meek." Mazza pried my hands off and she fell against the wall.

"I may have just woken up but I will have one of my cousins kill you." She looked over at all my male cousins and knew it was true. Lil Faz had the nerve to wave with his petty ass.

"Mazza can someone go and have her take a test? I need to make sure she's not lying."

"She did already Meek and it's true." Zia said with a sad face. They all loved C'Yani but we all knew if Theresa is pregnant and its mine, she'll never be with me again.

"I don't know what you're tryna prove but a baby won't keep me around. Now get the fuck out and I hope you fall down the steps and lose it."

"MEEK!" All the women shouted. Theresa walked out sad and holding her neck. I didn't give a fuck.

"Fuck her. It's my fault but I'm telling y'all I didn't let off in her." I explained and the women yelled but understood. All of us had to wait for her to deliver before we went any further. It's all we could do.

****

"You good cuz?" Shak came in and hugged me. I've been in here almost a week and couldn't wait to go home. I didn't even stay this long when that dumb bitch stabbed me.

"I'm alive. Thank you." I said to the nurse who wrapped the bandage around my stomach and pulled the covers up. I busted my stitches when I tried to squeeze the life outta Theresa that day and now they checked twice a day to make sure I'm healing right.

"I see you and Teri back together."

"Who told you that?"

"The smile on your face and the fact lil Faz mentioned her going to jail for whooping Barb's ass and you needing to

148

check on her. When no one heard back from you, we knew what it was."

"Yea a'ight."

"Y'all not together?"

"Yea but so what. Motherfuckers swear they know everything."

"You strung out nigga. It's all good."

"Whatever. Did C come back up?"

"Nah and I don't expect to see her. Especially with this bullshit Theresa pulling about being pregnant."

"Man, C'Yani was real hurt."

"What you mean?"

"From the looks of things, she rushed straight to the hospital when she heard. Then Theresa asked the doctor if you'll be fine to run after y'all baby. C stood and left. I went after her and she couldn't stop crying. All she kept saying was, she can't even be mad because y'all aren't together but why did you get her pregnant?" I let my head rest on the pillow thinking of how distraught she had to be.

"I need to see her." I was about to toss the covers off.

"Give it a few days and I'll try and get her up here." I nodded.

"In the meantime, me, Mazza and the rest of us are going to Connecticut in a few hours."

"Y'all can't wait?"

"You know we would but they fucked up and waiting isn't an option."

"A'ight. Hit me up soon as y'all get back."

"I will."

"Be safe. Love y'all." He said the same thing and reminded me of the security outside the door. They were being extra careful with me. I pressed the medication dispenser because the pain was kicking in, flipped through the channels and eventually dosed off.

"Stop crying C." He said and reached his hand out to me. It's been a over a week that he's been in the hospital so I decided to visit and find out why he did what he did. I moved over to the bed when I should've stayed put.

"Did I make you so angry it made you impregnate another woman?"

"Sit." He patted the seat next to him. As he slid over pain etched his face and I felt bad.

"I'm good." He held one of my hands in his.

"C'Yani, I fucked up. There's no other way around the situation."

"But why? Did I make you think I'd cheat on you or is it something I wasn't doing sexually?"

"None of that ma. I was mad at the video Kim showed me. I saw you on top of who I'm assuming is your ex and turned my back on you and for that I'm sorry. I should've waited and not allowed my anger to get the best of me."

"I understand how upset the video made you but why, or how could you even believe I'd do something like that? You know how I am?"

"I wasn't thinking."

"Do you love her?" I didn't want to hear the answer but I needed to know.

"Not at all. I care for her but that's it."

"You had unprotected sex with her, gave her a baby but you're not in love?"

"C, I know you're not used to things like this but yes it's what happened. I don't love her and I'm not even sure it's my child." I held my chest like an old woman clutching her pearls.

"I'm not about to go in detail because what she and I did doesn't concern you." I rolled my eyes but he's right.

"I was opening the condom, she went for a ride and I made her get up before I came."

"Do you know if the early stuff got inside?" I don't know why it was hard for me to talk dirty. He got a kick out of me because he laughed.

"I'm not sure if any pre-cum got in her but she's saying yes. C, I have to wait until she delivers and take a test. Look." He reached to wipe my eyes the best he could.

"I want you in my life and I can't apologize enough for what happened. However; I can't expect you to stick around but there is one thing you should be aware of before leaving." He fixed the covers on his legs.

"What's that?" I wiped my nose with some tissue off the tray.

"If you lie down with another man, I'll kill you." My eyes got big, heart started beating fast and my hands felt sweaty all of a sudden.

"Are you joking?"

"No and try me, to see if I will."

"But you slept with someone else."

"You heard what I said." I scooted back and he yelled out for security to come in the room.

"If anyone comes to my door tell them C is in here and either wait or come back later."

"It's ok. I'm leaving."

"No you're not." I had to get away from this maniac.

"We're not done. You can go." He told the guy and I tried to follow but security stopped and pushed me towards Meek. What in the hell is going on?

"I'm not gonna hurt you C. Come here." My feet were stuck to the ground.

"COME HERE!" He shouted and I jumped. Once the covers were tossed off his leg, I became extremely nervous. He's going to kill me in the hospital.

"If I get up you're gonna regret it."

"I already regret being with you." I thought I mumbled until he had me pushed against the wall.

"Too bad you can't take shit back." He lifted my shirt over my head, freed my breasts out of the bra and had me step out of my pants and underwear. Don't ask me why I didn't stop or even try to fight him. I was now fully naked and tried to cover myself but he smacked my hand away.

"I missed you." Two of his fingers bombarded their way inside my pussy while his thumb flickered over my

154

overgrown clit. Our mouths were now interacting with one another.

"Meekkkkkkkk." I couldn't hold it in and almost slid down the wall but he caught me.

"Still taste good. I have to sit ma." He moved to the chair, sat and lifted one of my legs on the arm of it.

"Meek someone may walk innnnnnnnnn. Oh dear God!!!!!" My hands gripped his head as that tongue of his did wonders in between my legs.

"Eat this pussy Meek. Just like that. Yesssss." So much of my nectar spit out, his face was covered. I allowed him to please me a few more times this way.

"Shit. My stomach is hurting but I gotta feel this banging ass pussy." Before I could protest he grabbed my waist, and slammed me down.

"I ain't never in my life had pussy this fucking good." He was kissing on my back and rubbing my breasts.

"You still love me C'Yani?" He yanked my hair with one hand and used the other to slam me up and down.

155

"Do you?" I didn't want to answer but he had a way of getting it out of me. He stood, bent me over the bed, pressed the button for the bed to go low, spread my pussy open and dog fucked the heck out of me.

"Answer my fucking question." His hands were on my shoulders, which pushed him further into me.

"Meek you hurt me." I started crying thinking about how he had another woman in this same position.

"Do you love me C'Yani?"

"Meek." He pulled out, flipped me over and sat me up.

"I'm so fucking sorry C. You are my everything and I'll never sleep with another woman again." I've never had a man kiss my tears away.

"I'm scared Meek."

"Don't be. I promise it won't happen again." I nodded as he reentered and pressed his lips on mine.

"I want you to have my baby C."

"I don't know. Oh my gawdddd, it feels good." I dug my nails in his back.

"I can't wait for you to have my kids." Our eyes met and I saw all the love he had for me in them.

"Shittttttt." His warm cum filled my walls.

"Luckily, you're on the pill because you'd damn sure be pregnant." He kissed my lips and held his hand out to help me up.

"You're bleeding." I pointed to his stomach.

"I'll take the pain and bleed anywhere if it means I can be inside you." He took my face in his two hands.

"I'm in love with you C'Yani Bailey and if you wanted my son or daughter I'd plant them in you with no problem, just to show you I mean everything I say." We stood there kissing.

"Mr. Gibson can we come in?" A woman yelled on the outside.

"Give me a few minutes. My woman is washing me up. I smirked as he held my hair up to watch me go down.

"I love you so fucking much C and I swear I'll never hurt you again. Got damn." I wrapped my lips on his huge dick and went to work.

"You're gonna make me cum C and I love watching you do it. Ahhhh fuckkkk." His body twitched and a few minutes later he moaned out my name and gave me all he had. I had him come in the bathroom, washed him up and made him sit on the chair with his leg up. His sheets needed to be changed.

"I love you too Meek but I'm gonna go and find someone to get even." I just wanted to see what he'd say. I grabbed my shoes and almost used the bathroom on myself again when the gun touched my forehead. Where the hell did he get one and why does he have it in here?

"I don't think you heard me the first time." He used the other hand to cock it and let me know the bullet is ready. I swallowed hard and put my hands up.

"If you lie with another man, I will fucking kill you. Do I make myself clear?" I nodded.

"I'm gonna give you some time to forgive me but know someone will be watching and unless it's your father coming over, I'll take it as you not listening and go from there."

"Meek?"

"Don't Meek me. The Baileys will be setting up your funeral sooner than later if you play with me." I smirked and grabbed my purse with him still pointing the gun at me.

"I'll never lie with another man but I needed you to feel how I felt hearing you laid down with another woman."

"WHAT?" He moved the gun off my forehead.

"Yea. I may not be a murderer or even a fighter but I do know how to hurt you. And that's by sleeping with someone else. Now I may die afterwards because as you stated you'll kill me. But at least you'll feel the pain you inflicted on me."

"C'Yani."

"I'm corny, but you taught me a lot in the bedroom and knowing I can show another man is killing you. And that's enough to make me feel a little even for your stupidity and the challenges this woman is gonna bring." I kissed his lips and walked to the door.

"C."

"I have to work around her Meek so thank you for giving me multiple obstacles to go through to be with you." I blew him a kiss and stepped out. Shak stood there grinning

159

with a few other family members. It's no secret they wanted us together and we will be, but it's a lot of things standing in our way that's for sure.

"Did you let him knock you up?" Big Faz said on the way out.

"I'm not ready for a child and until he knows if that woman is having a baby with him, he'll never get one from me." I shrugged my shoulders and pressed the elevator.

"Slowly but surely your blackness is seeping through. I have faith you'll show it soon." He pumped his fist for black power and went in the room. I loved Meek with all that I have but I won't tolerate him cheating when he gets mad. All the threats in the world won't make me stay

"Yo, I see your girl left." Shak strolled in the room popping shit.

"Whatever. I'm ready to go."

"Nigga you ain't been here that long."

"So. I'm not tryna sit here another day."

"Nah. Your ass tryna leave and make sure she don't sleep with someone else." Big Faz said and he was right. I needed to know C'Yani's every move. Men can play that I don't care roll all they want but not me. I care and refuse to allow another man to take her from me. I stood and pressed the button for the nurse to call the doctor.

"How'd it go in Connecticut?" I put my shirt on and hated the pain I'm in.

"Good. We got a few of his niggas but we haven't found him. All the places we assumed he'd run to, he didn't. Someone has to be hiding him."

"Yea because before all this he had no problem showing his face." Lil Faz strolled in.

"Exactly!" I slid my feet in the slippers my grandmother dropped off and picked my shit up to go.

"The doctor ain't been in here yet."

"I'll sign the papers at the desk." They followed me out and waited as the doctor gave me the reasons not to leave and then instructions since I am.

"Mr. Gibson please refrain from any activity that may bust your stitches open. An infection can set in and..."

"Yea. Yea. I got it. Peace." Shak pressed the elevator and just our luck Jasmine stepped on with Ty. I stared at the bitch and noticed her hair color. I grabbed her, lifted the shirt up and slammed her face into the elevator.

"Yo my man." I pulled my gun on Ty and held it in his face.

"Did you two motherfuckers attack my woman?" Shak, Faz and my other cousins looked and I heard the alarm go on from them stopping the elevator.

"What are you talking about?"

"Bitch you have the same color hair as my girl and same mole on your back as the chick in the video."

"What video?"

"Oh you playing dumb?" I hit Ty in the head and watched his eye split open again. I now had my gun under Jasmines chin.

When Kim showed me the video, I examined as much as possible. I've seen every inch of C'Yani's body and never noticed a mole. It didn't dawn on me then because of the rage filling up inside me but now that Jasmine's standing in front of me, resembling the fuck out my girl it makes sense. She probably had someone do it to make me think it's C.

"Who took that video?"

"I don't know what you're talking about?"

"You were in a hotel fucking him. Someone sent it to my ex pretending it was C'Yani. What the fuck you tryna do?"

"Ty and I are always in hotels."

"Are you ok in there?" Someone came over the intercom. The cameras were covered to block what I'm doing.

"We good." Shak yelled and big Faz told me to handle her another time.

"If I find out you attacked her, I swear I'm gonna kill you, him and everyone in your family. Stop fucking playing with me Jasmine." I tossed her on the other side of the elevator. Her stupid ass fell next to him as the doors opened.

"We stepped on and they were like this." Shak said and we stepped off giving her a look not to open her mouth.

"Why don't you kill her?"

"Did y'all forget her mother is the district attorney? My ass will be under the jail."

"Then it's time we turn it up a notch and get something on her mother. I'm sure she has some secrets we can use against her."

"We need to hurry up because she makes my ass itch every time I see her."

"It's all good but stop doing the shit in public." Big Faz popped me on my head.

"Take me home." They nodded and we all hopped in the car. I had enough shit for today.

****

"What the fuck?" I woke up to the smoke alarm going off in my house. I ran down the steps as fast as I could and almost fell because my leg isn't fully healed.

"Who the hell?" I stepped in the kitchen and smoke was clouding the kitchen. I turned the stove off and the bacon was burnt. I tossed the pan in the sink, turned the vent on and used the dishrag to fan some of the smoke. I noticed the back door opened and went to it. I looked around the entire back yard and no one was there.

Ding Dong. The doorbell ringing brought me in. I locked the door and went to see who came over.

"What up?" Shak stepped in and asked me what I cooked.

"Someone broke in and..."

"And what?" He pulled his gun out and started checking the rooms downstairs.

"I can't even tell you but I can't stay here being outta commission."

"How they get in!"

"I literally woke up from the fire detector."

165

"Check the cameras."

"Oh shit. That's right." We ran in my office and turned them on.

"This bitch." We watched Kim pick the lock and disable my alarm somehow. She observed the house with a grin and rubbed her stomach. She was talking to herself on the camera about me being happy she's having a baby and some other shit. The bitch must've really gotten pregnant by my pops or went out and fucked someone else.

"Yoooo!" He shouted when she removed a photo of me and my pops off the fireplace and played with herself until she came. The nasty bitch rubbed her pussy up and down the couch like a dog and smelled it.

"I know."

"I had no idea she was that crazy."

"Me neither in the beginning."

The two of us watched her go up the steps, in my room and stare at me. It pissed me off because had I not been high off the medication, I would've felt her presence. She stepped out, closed the door and went downstairs in the kitchen to cook.

All she got was the bacon started because her phone rang and she forgot. You could see panic on her face as she attempted to keep the alarm from going off. Once it did, she ran out the house.

"What you gonna do?"

"I have no idea where she could be hiding and why the fuck she can't let go." I stood and went to make sure the smoke was going away.

"Can't you stay with C?"

"I can but I'm not."

"Why?"

"I told her I'm gonna give her time to forgive me. It won't happen if I'm with her because I'ma fuck her any chance I get to make her pregnant."

"How she go from not being able to fuck to stringing your ass out?" I laughed.

"I can't even tell you. The first time we had sex she was clueless as fuck. I mean she had no fucking idea what to do as far as being on top, from behind or even going down. Dude, wasn't fucking her right at all." He shook his head.

"As the days went on she became persistent in learning and started taking notes off websites and shit. Before I knew it, she was teaching me things."

"And now you can't let go."

"Fuck you nigga. I'm staying with you until Kim is found."

"You still got the key right?"

"Yea."

"Good. I'll help you move some of yo shit, then I have to deal with Teri."

"What happened?"

"One minute we were on the same page about moving in. She goes out with Jasmine and comes home claiming I'm controlling her.

"Jasmine told her that?"

"Yup. That's why we need to get rid of her ASAP. Oh, and she almost told Teri you fucked her."

"Say what?" He explained how she came over talking about secrets and shit. It's not that C'Yani didn't have the right to know. I just feel like she's my past and there's no need to say anything about it. Neither of them care for the other so it's not like she can feel some kind of way. I just wanna keep my girl from all pain but Jasmine is tryna hurt her and I'm not having it. I'm gonna figure out something to get rid of her and Kim if it's the last thing I do.

"Shit. Shit. Shit." I heard the alarm go off and hauled ass out Meek's house. My intention was to make him breakfast and leave. Granted, I would've loved to climb in bed with him but I'm sure he'd most likely kill me.

Meek isn't the type of man who plays a lotta games with women. He's gentle, loving, will spoil the hell outta his woman and his love making will have a bitch going crazy. Hence; the very reason I can't leave him alone. He fucked my entire life up and not in a good way. Let me tell you what I mean.

He entered my life at the gym by bumping into me. He's a big guy and excused himself. I instantly began flirting and he took the bait. We went on a date and a bitch was hooked right away and that's just off conversation. He isn't your average street dude who ain't about shit. He's definitely a hood nigga but he's smart.

I learned he owned a construction company and had his hands in other investments. The conversations we shared were not only informative but intelligent. I would become so fascinated by his words, I'd bring up dumb shit just to hear him speak.

As far as the sex goes. Let's just say I refuse to allow another woman to experience the pleasure he's given me. The way he takes his time to please a woman is what I love the most. Men these days don't take the time out to figure a woman's likes and dislikes. They just hop on top, fuck the way they want and keep it moving.

For instance, if it were a position I didn't like, he'd stop and try a different one. Or we'd try it again but he'd go slower and ask if I'm ok. I've never had a man eat my pussy the way he does either. The currents flow through your body like you've been struck by lightning. What I mean is, it's so electrifying that it'll make a bitch crazy, which is exactly how he made me. Now he's tryna get rid of the woman he created. Like how you mad?

Anyway, my sister told me about the little stuck up bitch who's been visiting him at the company. She's not sure if they had sex in the office but if they did, hell yea I'm mad. He never sexed me in there and trust I tried because of the building.

171

It's high up and the view is beautiful. I wanted to stare out as he fucked me from behind.

Nevertheless, my sister and her old associate whooped her ass and once Meek witnessed the video, anger filled him and I was ecstatic. He wouldn't be with her anymore and a bitch was happy but now I had to deal with the other trick claiming to be pregnant.

I found that out because Mia still talks to people at the job and the woman has been up there to see him. Supposedly, he wasn't in but told his secretary to remind him about the baby's doctor appointment. It's all good because I'm positive the kid ain't his. He's not the type to get caught slipping but you never know. If she is pregnant by him, then I'll have to get rid of her too.

"Where you at?" I hopped in my car and sped off down the street praying Meek didn't come running out and catch me.

"Home." Mia answered.

"I'll be right there."

"The door is open." I hung up and drove straight there. I walk in and there's the other bitch who used to fuck him. I gave her a fake smile and she did the same.

"Let me talk to you." I grabbed my sisters' arm and went in the bedroom.

"What happened and why do you smell like burnt bacon?" I explained and she fell out laughing.

"How's my niece or nephew?" She rubbed my belly. Neither of us noticed her nosy ass friend come in.

"Oh shit. Meek got you pregnant too?" The bitch had a grin on her face. Mia said, all she wanted to do is make C'Yani hurt for being stuck up. To me it's a stupid ass reason but that's her shit.

"If you must know, yes." I told my sister, I snuck in, handcuffed him to the bed and had sex until he came in me a few times. All of it's true, except the part of it being Meek but who cares? They don't need to know the full details. The DNA is still the same because it's his fathers. It will be Meek's sibling but again, who cares?

"Girl yes. She handcuffed him and fucked until he let off." Mia shouted.

"I ain't even mad at you. At least the baby will be set for life."

"You got that right." I rubbed my belly and looked out the window when I heard a car screech.

"Who is that?" Mia and Jasmine rushed to the window.

"Oh that's Charlie."

"MIAAAAAAA!" He shouted and you could hear him opening doors looking for her.

"In here babe." He busted in and the look on his face was not a happy one.

"You ok?" He grabbed her by the neck and slammed her against the window.

"Did you steal my keys, turn off the video in my office and attack some woman at the hotel?" Mia nodded her head no.

"You're fucking lying."

"I'm not lying and why you yoking me up?"

"Do you know those niggas went to my mother's spot and beat up my brother and two cousins looking for me. They think I set the shit up." He banged Mia's head on the wall.

"Get yo hands off her." Jasmine hit him in the back of the head with a lamp. He let go and stumbled.

"Let me guess. I bet you were with her." Mia stood there tryna catch her breath as Jasmine stared him down.

"Is that where the expensive stuff came from because I damn sure didn't buy it?" He pulled some bags out the closet with Gucci and Prada on it.

"Charlie."

"Charlie my ass bitch. My brother is only 17 and my two cousins are 18 and 20. They put them in the hospital." All of us covered our mouth.

"I don't know what type of shit you on but believe me when I say, I'm telling." Jasmine went to hit him again and he knocked the shit outta her.

"I really loved you Mia but I can't be with a woman who steals and attacks a female over whatever and leaves her to die. I'm out." He slammed the door and a minute later you heard him pulling off.

"We have to go." I told her and helped pack a few bags.

"We have to wake her up." She pointed to Jasmine laid out on the ground.

"Not our problem." I grabbed her and took her to the place I've been hiding out at. It's the only way to remain safe.

"Don't worry sis. We'll come up with a plan to get this C'Yani bitch. Her time is coming." I drove off with many thoughts in my head of how to get her. She's not gonna know what hit her by the time I'm done.

"TERI!" I shouted and tossed my keys on the table. I came over to talk because this shit with her and Jasmine is getting on my fucking nerves. I'd never ask her to choose her friends but something's gotta give. I can't have my woman listening to a hateful and jealous bitch.

"YO TERI! WE NEED TO..." I stopped dead in my tracks and smiled. This woman knew she had my heart and anything else she wanted. She had soft music playing and looked sexy as fuck.

"I missed you and I'm sorry for being standoffish lately." She moved closer to me in the fuck me heels and tassels hanging from her breasts.

"What else?" I lifted my arms to assist her in removing my shirt.

"I'm sorry for holding out on what you love the most." She unzipped my jeans and used her small hands to guide them down along with my boxers.

"Who said I was giving you some?"

"He did." She pointed to my man sticking straight up.

177

"Then I suggest you talk to him." She kneeled down in a squatting position and took me in her mouth. It's been about a week since I felt any sort of sexual pleasure so any touch is bound to have me ready to nut right away.

"I swear you're the best T. Fuckkkk!" I moaned out and let her drain me for all I had. She trailed soft kisses up my body and sucked on my sides as well. She knew how much I enjoyed her pleasing me and never complained. Once our lips connected, I lifted her in my arms and laid her gently on the bed.

"I love you so much Shakim." I smiled and threw my tongue in her mouth again. I placed my mouth on her titties and began sucking on them. She had her hand on my head as I roughly bit down on the nipple.

"Yes baby." I went further and spread her legs apart.

"You sexy as hell in these heels baby." I kissed inside her thighs.

"Only for you." I had a grin on my face staring up at her as my tongue dove deep in her pussy. She arched her back and began grinding on my face. I stuck two fingers inside, placed my mouth on her clit and brought her to ecstasy.

"SHAKIMMMMMM!" Her body continued to shake as I finger fucked, twirled my tongue around and ate her pussy like it was my last meal.

"Fuck, you taste good." I crashed my lips on hers again and played at her entrance.

"What's that?" I asked and turned toward the door. I didn't bother closing it because it's her house and no one was here.

"I didn't hear anything." She grabbed my face and told me to put it in.

I put the tip at her entrance and felt her juices seeping out. I pushed further in and her muscles were clamping down. I lifted her legs on my shoulders and went as deep as I could. Both of us let out a moan. The more I pounded, the more she scratched and moaned. I didn't care because it only meant I'm doing my job.

"Don't ever give this dick away. Got damn you feel so good baby." I had her sit up and turn around.

"Daddy ain't going nowhere. Shitttttt." I slid in from behind and had to stop myself from cumming.

"Throw it back T." She did and I heard the same noise as before. It sounded like someone moaning and it wasn't Teri. I turned to the door again and instantly got mad. This bitch had one leg up, leaning on the door as she played in her pussy.

"Tha fuck!" I tried to stop but Teri threw it back harder. I turned around to tell Teri but couldn't because she made me cum hard as fuck.

"I'm gonna be sick." Teri said jumping off and running in the bathroom. I wanted to go behind her but needed to deal with this shit.

"Yo." I snatched the bitch up by her hair. I was so fucking mad, I didn't even care my ass was still naked. She didn't scream or make any noise, which let me know Teri had no idea she came in.

"Get the fuck out." Jasmine smirked and reached out to stroke my dick. I pushed her dumb ass right down the steps. Unfortunately, the bitch didn't die so I snatched her by the ankles and drug her to the door.

"Shakim what are you doing?" I heard Teri ask and looked up to see her covered in a robe.

"Sis, I came over to see you and he tried to fuck me. I told you he wasn't shit."

"What?"

"I didn't know y'all were having sex and walked past the room. He told me to come in and I didn't. When y'all finished, he grabbed me and was about to take it."

"WHAT BITCH!" I had my foot on her face. I was about to stomp the fuck out this bitch but I remembered Meek telling me who her mother is. We had to be careful with handling her.

"Shakim please tell me it's not true." I saw her eyes getting watery.

"Teri how the fuck you sound. I just finished having sex with you. You think I'm gonna risk everything we got for a ho? Are you serious?"

"Why aren't you covered up then?" She folded her arms.

"I told you I heard something earlier T. It was her watching and she tried to join when I was fucking you." She looked at both of us. Right before Teri jumped off she started walking towards me. I guess this bitch knew my background and assumed I'd do a threesome but that would never happen with my girl.

"You know what? I'm done." I stomped on her face anyway and ran up the steps to get my things.

"Shakim."

"Teri, I told you before the bitch is sneaky. I'm not about to stand here and watch you decide who to believe."

"I didn't say I believed her." I zipped my jeans up and searched for my shirt.

"The minute you asked me to say it's not true, is when you second guessed it."

"Baby please." I heard the pain in her voice.

"What T? Is it the baby?"

"No, I just don't want you to leave me." I pulled her close to me.

"I'm not leaving you but we need some space right now. You obviously wanna keep your friend around and have me. I hate to be the nigga to say this but it's either her or me." I kissed her forehead, picked my shirt up off the ground and left the room.

"This the shit I'm talking about T." Jasmine was standing outside the door listening.

"Move bitch before I throw your ass out the fucking window."

"Shakim don't talk to me like that." I wrapped my hand around her throat.

"I should kill you for what you did."

"What else did she do Shakim?" I could hear confusion from my girl.

"All I'm gonna say is, she ain't your friend." I banged the bitch head against the wall and walked down the steps.

"Her or me Teri." I slammed the door and jumped in my car. I sent a message to my cousins and told them to meet me at the club.

****

"Hold up! The bitch watched y'all?" Meek asked after slamming his shot glass down on the bar.

"Hell yea. Teri jumps up to use the bathroom and me trying not to let her see what the dumb bitch did, I drug her out the room and threw her down the steps."

"Yo! I expected for Kim to do some shit like that but Jasmine? She tryna fuck you?" I threw back a shot.

"I don't know and you know we don't even roll like that."

"What you wanna do?"

"I left Teri and told her she had to make a choice." Lil Faz sat there shaking his head.

"I ain't try to give her an ultimatum but there's no way we can both exist in Teri's world."

"What she say?"

"Cried and asked me not to leave."

"Y'all niggas got the craziest bitches I've ever seen. I swear my mom watch stories like this on Lifetime."

"Fuck you nigga." I tossed back another shot

"I'm serious and Meek, Kim ass definitely watched too much Thin Line Between Love and Hate. Remember that bitch broke in the house and burnt bacon?" He shook his head laughing.

"The only thing next is a dead rabbit in a pot like on fatal attraction."

"Let me find out you watch those crazy movies too."

"Hell yea I do. I'm preparing myself for the signs. I ain't tryna deal with this shit."

"Nigga didn't you say the bitch from C'Yani job stalking you?" I busted out laughing. The two of us fucked these bitches who were around 30 and the one chick I left alone. The other one is strung out on Faz or something.

"That's because I put this Chambers dick in her life. You know my mom almost beat her ass when she showed up. Fazira came out and walked the dogs with her. Pops had to pull her off." Fazira is his twin sister and she may not be able to stand his ass like most siblings but she plays no games when it comes to her family.

"Cuz didn't record it?"

185

"Nah because he didn't know at first." All of us laughed and continued drinking.

"I would've loved to see that."

"Yea well the bitch can definitely suck dick but that pussy wasn't as good." He shrugged his shoulders and sipped on his beer.

"A'ight y'all, I'm out." I started feeling dizzy and plus a few bitches I fucked came strolling in barely dressed. I had to go, otherwise; my dick will be caught up somewhere it didn't belong. I looked down at my phone and saw the text from Teri saying she loved me. Its definitely confirmation that I needed to get my ass up outta here.

"I'm gone too." Both of my cousins walked out behind me and went their separate ways. I drove home with thoughts of killing Barb in the morning and making sure we find out some information Jasmine's mother. The bitch has got to go.

I stared at Jasmine when Shakim walked out and seeing the way she fidgeted with her hands, let me know something wasn't right. People may think I'm naive to the shit she does and I'm not. However; we're all grown and they can address her themselves. Everyone expects me to say something and I get it but if they're handling it, why would I? The shit with my sister is different though because like I said, she never comes for C in front of me.

I told Jasmine I'd be right back and jumped in the shower. It was late as hell which is another reason I'm about to dig in her ass. Why is she even at my house? Better yet; why you watching me and my man have sex?

I absolutely believed Shakim when he accused her of doing it. He's never lied to me, even when it hurt so why would he now. It bothered me how he gave me an ultimatum but I understand why. This isn't the first time he mentioned her ruining things between me and the people I love. Hell, she's the exact reason my own sister won't speak to me.

187

I locked my bedroom door, started the shower and handled my business. All I kept thinking of, is how she entered my house in the first place? Shakim and my family are the only ones who had a key. I know she didn't break in because the alarm didn't go off. The thing frustrating me now is her watching. Never in all the years I've known her, has she done anything remotely dumb.

I threw my clothes on and walked down stairs to hear her yelling on the phone. Instead of listening, I grabbed my keys and went to the door; gesturing for her to come too. She picked her things up and followed me out. I locked the door and walked to my car.

"Where you going?" She asked hanging the phone up.

"To see my man."

"Wait! I know you're not still considering being with him after what he did?" I tossed my purse and phone in my car and stood face to face with her.

"Why are you here?"

"What?" She had the nerve to look offended.

"You heard me. It's after one in the morning and you're at my house. You didn't call and mention an emergency so I'm gonna ask again. Why are you here?" She stood there stuck on stupid and I had to laugh.

"Never mind. How did you get in?"

"The door was unlocked." It may have been because a few times before he forgot to lock it.

"I didn't hear you knock or the doorbell."

"What you tryna say Teri?"

"I've let a lotta shit slide with you Jasmine because you're my friend. But don't get it fucked up. If I find out you had anything to do with my sister being attacked, I'm gonna beat your ass like it's never been done before."

"What the hell does your sister have to do with me stopping by? And since when you start choosing a nigga over me?"

"Because ever since she's been attacked I haven't really seen you." She couldn't debate that because it's true. We hung out all the time but after the shit with Barb and C, she distanced herself from me. Yea, she stopped by a few times but not like the normal.

"Oh, and I chose him the second he put that good ass dick in my life." I walked to my car.

"I hope you enjoyed the show because trust me, it's definitely worth all the moaning I did." I opened the door.

"Make this your last time showing up in the middle of the night."

"Are you serious?"

"Dead serious. My man's dick belongs to me and I'm the only one who should be seeing, touching and tasting it."

"You and every other bitch out here he's been with." I laughed.

"He may have fucked those women but can't no bitch tell you they had him in love or got them pregnant."

"You're bragging on a man who dips out each time y'all argue?"

"Don't worry about what the fuck he does? Wait a minute?" I stormed back over to her as she tried to rush getting in the car.

"Did you fuck him?" She smirked.

"Not at all but after seeing how big his dick is, I damn sure would."

I don't know what came over me. I started raining blows all over her face. Jasmine is no match for me and she knows it, which is why she never got on my bad side. I grabbed her head and banged it into the side of the car. When she fell, my foot connected with her stomach as I stomped her the fuck out. Once I got tired, I kneeled down next to her and lifted her head. Blood poured out her mouth and nose.

"Make that the last time you mention my man's dick. Matter of fact, erase any memory you had of seeing it because if I assume you're fantasizing about my nigga, next time I'm gonna kill you." I slammed her head in the ground. I've never taken a life but my shooting game on point from the gun range. I'll do anything to protect my family and now that he's a part of it, I'll do whatever's necessary.

****

Instead of going to Shakim's, I drove to my parents and went in. I thought about calling him but decided to let him cool off. Plus, if I went to see him he'd punish me and my pussy is sore as hell. I did send him a text saying I love you and I'll see him soon. He read it and sent the same thing back.

"Hey honey. What are you doing here?" My father walked in and sat on my bed.

"That girl is a piece of work." He shook his head after listening to me explain what went down at my house.

"I know. How's C'Yani?"

"She's good. Just worried about Mekhi. You know she loves him." My father called him by his government, while my mom called him by the street name.

"Oh, she took him back?"

"I don't think so but once she heard about him being shot she went to the hospital."

"He got some chick pregnant and your sister isn't taking it well. Teri, you should go see her." My mom said leaning on the door.

"Pregnant?" My mom came and laid in the bed next to me.

"When he thought your sister slept with Ty, he went out and had sex with some woman. Anyway, she came to the hospital and revealed they were expecting. C'Yani was crushed."

"I bet she was." I couldn't imagine what she was going through and didn't want to. I would probably kill Shakim if he did some crazy shit like that to me.

Listening to the situation only made me wanna be next to my man more. I kissed both of them, put my shoes on, grabbed my things and drove to his house. At first, I was a little nervous about going in because what if he didn't wanna see me, or tried to make me leave? Ignoring all that, I used my key and went inside. I smiled at the few photos he had of us on the fireplace. I wanted to put them in my house but he said since I'll be moving in soon they needed to be here.

"What you doing here?" I felt his hands wrap around my waist and land on my stomach.

"I didn't wanna sleep without you." He turned me around and stared.

"I'm not the type of nigga to pass out ultimatums but it ain't gonna work with her in your life."

"I know and I'm sorry for questioning you. In my heart, I knew she did it because you've never lied to me."

"She must want some of daddy dick." He placed a kiss on my neck.

"It's exactly what she said before I beat her ass." He stopped kissing me and pulled away.

"After you left, I took a shower and confronted her. At first, she denied it by accusing me of listening to you, but when she mentioned your size I lost it on her."

"Let's go." He grabbed his car keys and led me out the door.

"Where we going?"

"To the ER. You fought that bitch for disrespecting you and me and I get it. But don't think for one minute she didn't know how you'd react." He opened the door for me.

"What you mean?"

"Ma, she wants you to lose the baby."

"I don't think so." He pulled off.

"Think about it T. She accused me of tryna control you, then showed up at your spot and watched us have sex. Never mind all the times she told you I'm no good and let's not forget she's mad about you moving in. She knows I won't let her come over and now that you're having my baby, she knows it's a wrap." I laid my head on the seat and thought about what he said. He pulled in the parking lot and held my hand when we got out.

"My girl was in a fight and needs to be checked because she's pregnant." He told the receptionist who sent us upstairs. The nurse had me get undressed and I called my parents to let them know I'm here.

"Ok, let's see what we have going on." The doctor walked in smiling and proceeded to do the test.

"Look here mommy and daddy. There's your little one." Shakim jumped up and smiled staring at the screen. This is the first time he's seen our baby. I had a sonogram photo but its not the same as being there.

"Is that his dick because it looks big like mine?"

"SHAKIM!" I shouted and the doctor turned beet red.

"Sir, we have to wait another month before we can find out the sex of the baby."

"I don't care what you say. That's his dick and he about to have the bitches going crazy like his dad. Let me get a picture doc."

"Please excuse him. His rude cousins and uncle raised him."

"Don't come for my peoples Teri. Wait til I tell them what you said."

"Shakim I don't feel like dealing with them."

"Too late." He took his phone out and sent a picture to everyone's phone in a group text.

"Ok mommy. The baby looks fine but I do suggest you keep the stress level down and contact your doctor in the morning." I nodded and he told me to stay for another hour or two just to be safe.

"Damn T, you about to give me a baby." He leaned down and kissed me.

"Please don't hurt me Shak."

"Never babe. You're the only woman I want in my life. Damn, I got a fucking kid on the way. Can we start shopping?" I think he was more excited than me.

"Shakim, I'm scared."

"Don't be T. If you want, I'll go out and buy the monitor thing that goes on your stomach. You can listen all day if you want." I nodded and he wiped my eyes.

"What happened to your sister is fucked up but baby try not to think about it."

"Ok."

"Now let me see what all the hype is about."

"Huh?"

"Niggas always talking about seeing their women pussy under the GYN light and since you're the only one I've ever been with in this position, I wanna see." He closed the door, clicked the light on and spread my legs.

"It looks good ma and my baby is gonna come out and fuck this pussy up." I closed my legs and he spread them back open.

"I'm saying. Your pussy is gonna be wide open. I don't think I can see it because it will contaminate this image right here. Shit, let me take a picture." He did it and a few seconds later I felt his tongue on my clit.

"Baby."

"Cum for your man." I couldn't hold it in as he brought me to a pleasure, I've encountered from him on more than one occasion.

"I can't wait to have you waking up to me everyday." He wiped me down and just as I was about to give him head, the doctor walked in and discharged me.

"I think he heard you moaning." Shak handed me my clothes.

"Why you say that?"

"Because its only been an hour and he wanted you to stay for two." We both started laughing.

"I love you Shakim and I'm glad you're gonna be my baby daddy."

"Baby daddy? Nah, we're gonna get married because I can't have my child being a bastard baby coming out."

"Shakim."

"What? They say when you not married it's what a kid is called outta wedlock." I walked ahead of him to the car and got in. My man is crazy but I won't trade him in for no one.

"She good." I told Teri's mom on the phone. After we left the hospital, she went straight to sleep.

"Ok. Well make sure she eats and drinks a lot of water Shakim." I smiled listening to her tell me how to care for Teri. The Baileys loved the hell outta their kids and wanted nothing but the best for them so I get it.

"I will."

"Shakim try and get her to speak with C'Yani. My daughter is taking it really hard over Meek."

"I know and he loves her."

"Oh, you don't have to tell me. He's been calling trying to get me to speak to her. I told him to take his ass up to her job and make her." I laughed because it's no doubt in my mind he's going to do it. We spoke a little longer and hung up.

I walked in the bedroom and noticed Teri bunched up on my side of the bed. It's funny because I have a California King, yet; she never gives me my own space. She can be on her side when I first walk in but by the time I wake up, her ass is so far under me, I'm almost hanging off the bed. I guess that's what good dick does to you.

I sat next to her and stared as she slept. I never in a million years thought a woman could make me settle. Having different pussy, in different area codes is living the life. But when that special woman comes in your life, sacrificing those things you love the most is the only way to keep the peace. She's definitely worth it though. That's why I'm gonna make sure Barb gets what's coming to her as well as Jasmine. I'm not gonna kill her because my cousin wants to but she's gonna feel my wrath for sure.

"Hey baby." Teri spoke after opening her eyes.

"How you feel?" I ran my hand down her face.

"I'm ok. You leaving?" I leaned down and placed a kiss on her lips.

"Yea. I got some things to handle."

"Shakim, I don't want them breaking none of my things." She told me last night that she'd move in with me and would start packing today. I told her a moving company would do it, to alleviate any stress or lifting. Her concern about losing

201

or even having a stillborn baby is weighing heavy on her and I understand. If there's any way to make sure she doesn't stress, you damn right I'm gonna do it.

"I'm gonna take you there to grab your personal things, so if you want other stuff grab it. The rest the movers will bring here. What you wanna do about your furniture?" I took my clothes off to go shower.

"I'm going to rent the place out so the living room and guest bedroom stuff can stay. My bedroom stuff you can toss, I guess. I don't want anyone sleeping on the mattress my man had me on." I heard her say from the bedroom.

"What you doing T?" I watched her step in the shower and smiled at her pouch.

"I've been thinking about you saying we should get married."

"Oh yea." I had my head leaning on the shower wall as her hands gently stroked my man to life.

"Yea. When do yo wanna do it?" She started teasing my dick with her tongue.

"Whenever. Oh shit T." She swallowed me and a nigga enjoyed the show. Teri is a beast at giving me head and watching her is a bonus. I love how nasty she gets.

As she bobbed her head, I could hear her spit. She knew I love that extra shit. Her hands wrapped around my dick, as she placed every inch in her mouth. I wrapped her hair around and made love to her mouth. The moment my dick twitched and she knew I was ready, she went crazy and I think it's one of the hardest times I've ever cum. Which is the exact reason I had to get my shit together because no other man will ever experience this pleasure and if they did, I'd kill both of them.

"Damn, I needed that." I helped her stand, turned her around and had her screaming out my name. Say what you want but hearing a woman yell out in pleasure only makes the man go harder and its exactly what I did.

"You ready for this dick?" I kissed the back of her neck. I had her hands on the wall and the front of her facing it.

"Yes baby." I plunged inside and knew she came just that quick because her body became even weaker.

I lifted her leg and held it in the crook of my arm. The moans were sexy and so was the way she let her ass clap for me. I had the perfect woman in my bed, sexing me and giving me my first child. The only thing left to do is marry her.

Her hand reached behind my head and brought us close to indulge in a tongue fight. The craving for one another was outta this world and no one could tell us different.

"Hold on T." I shut the shower off, carried her in the bedroom and made love to her off and on all day. If this is how the rest of my life is gonna be, I'll take it.

****

"Its about time you called me back." Tasha said when I walked in the house. She had been hitting me up like crazy since the shit with Barb.

When Teri broke up with me, I didn't go to her. I slept with other bitches who would be easy to break it off with because I knew Teri would come back. Especially; after constantly nagging my family. I still get a kick outta Lil Faz and Mystic teasing me over it. They'll know soon enough what it's like being love and it'll be me teasing their ass.

"What up and where she at?" I got straight to the point. I wasn't here to fuck or anything else. I wanted to get this shit done and over with.

"In the shower but wait." I stopped from going up the steps.

"Can I have you one last time?" I chuckled at her stupidity. I let her know from gate we'd never fuck again. If anyone knew how I felt about someone asking me the same shit over and over, it's the three bitches who used to live with me and being she's one of them, she definitely knows.

"Nah. My girl got this dick on lock."

PHEW! I watched her body drop to the ground and sent a text to my people to come for two clean ups.

See when I returned Tasha's call, I didn't think she'd give Barb up. However; once I mentioned her being able to reap the benefits with a large amount of money, she sung like a canary. I had no clue where Barb went after leaving the hospital and with Teri breaking up with me, I forgot to look into it. I'm not saying I didn't care but my cousins were hit too and it was a lotta shit going on in general.

I made my way up the steps and heard Barb singing in the shower with no care in the world. I opened the door and leaned on the wall waiting for her to finish. I could've murked her right here, but I wanted to ask a few questions and make sure my face is the last one she saw before meeting her maker. A few minutes later the water shut off and she reached for a towel. I handed it to her and smirked at the look on her face after seeing me. Fear was evident and it should be. Barb knows I don't play games so if I'm here she knows what it is.

"What did you do to my girls' car?" She stood there dripping wet. Usually my dick would get hard but because this is a death call and Teri has my shit on lock, my man ain't move.

"What are you doing here?" Tears rolled down her face.

"My girl's car. What did you do to it?"

"I didn't do anything." I pushed her against the wall and her head bounced off it.

"Tha fuck you do?"

"I had a computer guy mess with the technology in the car. He was able to make the gas leak from the exhaust pipe." I couldn't believe she went through the extreme to remove Teri outta my life.

"Why?"

"Because you were our man Shak."

"Bitch, I have never been your man."

"Yes you were. You took care of us, fucked us, gave us money if needed and a car. We were your number one. How the fuck you let her come in and…" I didn't even let her finish because she sounded stupid as fuck.

"When a man claims a chick as his own it will only be one. There were three of you here and I fucked all of you plus others. So go ahead with you thought this or that." I backed away and watched her pick the towel up.

"Shak, why didn't you pick me? I would've…" I stepped out the room with her hair wrapped around my hand. I drugged her down the steps kicking and screaming. Once she saw Tasha's body on the ground she threw up. It didn't matter to me because she's about to suffer the same fate she attempted to bestow on my girl.

"Get in." She did like I asked, unaware of what I had planned. I nodded at my boy standing in the corner and listened to the doors lock and the car start. Barb, stared out the window and tried to open the door.

"You're not the only one with connections." I smirked. Me and the guy stepped out the garage at the same time Tasha's body was being placed in the black van. I turned to see Barb banging on the window, yelling with tears coming down her face. With no remorse, I smiled at my girl who was in my car waiting. She wanted to take her life, but I'm making sure she does absolutely nothing during this pregnancy.

"How much longer?" My peoples asked. Ten minutes passed and we were positive Barb was gone.

"You can do it now." He and I both got in our cars and pulled off.

"Press the button bae." I said to Teri and once she did, the entire house blew up. See, I could've shot Barb in the head but I wanted her to stare death in the face like my girl did. The only difference is no one saved her.

I had my girl blow her house up to feel like she had a part in taking her life. Also, the fire department will think she committed suicide. My stepfather may have the police on his side but I also didn't wanna jeopardize his position or theirs by doing too much.

"I'm gonna fuck the shit outta you tonight babe." Teri grabbed my face to hers at the stop light and we went at it like we do at home. It wasn't until someone blew that we stopped.

"Well let me get us home and let you do just that." I drove off thinking of the nasty things we're about to do to one another. *This is the fucking life.*

"I'm here for C'Yani." I told the woman at the receptionist desk. She was still working at her other job until the CO and other inspections went through in the building she brought. I've come a few times to pick her up but never stayed long. She didn't want the women staring at me. Too bad she won't have a choice today.

"Who may I say is here?"

"Bitch you know who I am. You've seen me here before. Don't fucking play with me." The white woman became flustered and I didn't care.

"Fuck this. I know where her office at and I wish you would call security or the cops." I shouted and pressed the elevator. When the doors opened I stepped on and used my finger to light up the floor I'm going to.

"I never get tired of looking at his fine ass." I heard the second I stepped off.

"Hell no. Who he here for though because Theresa said she's having a baby by him. I know boss lady ain't dealing with that." I turned to see the two gossiping bitches standing there staring.

"Hey baby." I swung my head and Theresa came towards me with her arms out for a hug. I put my hand out and mushed the shit outta her. I could hear the laughs.

"Meek, you play too much."

"Bitch, I ain't playing but I see you full of games. Let me put you up on something." I pushed her against the wall but not too hard and squeezed her cheeks.

"If you continue fucking with my girl I'm gonna make sure you come up missing." C still wasn't speaking or seeing me and it's been two and a half weeks. She did send me a text yesterday asking me to talk to my baby momma about the disrespect and childish behavior she did at work. Her words, not mine.

"Meek, how could you manhandle me with our child in my stomach?"

"Bitch stop putting a show on for these ho's."

"Ho's?" One of the gossiping chicks asked.

211

"Yea ho's. Aren't you the bitch my cousin fucked in the hotel not too long ago. Then called him crying because he put you on knock off now that he's back with his woman. And you." I pointed to the other one.

"Doing threesomes and shit with my little cousin. You're like what 30 and he's 19 turning you the fuck out. Don't show up at his mom's house again begging to see him. She's not one to fuck with." I redirected my attention back to Theresa.

"Stay the fuck away from me."

"Meek."

"Fuck outta here." I mushed her and listened as her head hit the wall.

"I told y'all heffa's he ain't the man you wanna piss off." C'Yani's secretary said and I winked at her. She's cool as hell and leaving when C is.

"I didn't tell her you're here."

"Good. I like surprising her."

"Oh, she's gonna be surprised alright." She smirked.

"It better not be no other nigga in there."

"Boy please. She ain't never getting over you." I heard someone suck their teeth.

"Don't do it Meek. Go see your woman." She opened the door and I gave all those bitches a hateful stare.

"Everything will be ready and sent over by messenger shortly." C'Yani spoke on the phone with her back turned. I locked her door and moved towards her.

"You as well sir." I stood behind her and placed a kiss on her neck.

"Have a good day." She let the earpiece fall out and turned around.

"I guess you're here to handle your baby momma." I laughed at her being angry.

"Get over here." She went to grab a water out the fridge.

"I'm fine." I smiled and removed my shirt on the way to her.

"Meek put your shirt on."

"I will later." I kicked my shoes off, let my jeans slide down and stood in front of her in my boxers and wife beater.

"Did you miss me?" I had both of my arms on the wall above her head. She bit down on her lip and then cleared her throat.

"Why are you here?" I used my two fingers to make her look in my eyes.

"How much longer until you're back in my bed?" I planted a soft kiss on her lips.

"When you find out if that's your kid."

"Bullshit!" I ripped her blouse opened and yanked it off her body. If she wanted to play tough, I'm about to show her tough.

"Meek you ripped my shirt." She whined. I swung her around to face the wall, unsnapping her bra at the same time.

"Mmmmm." I heard her moan as my hands caressed both of her breasts from behind.

"You tryna hold this pussy hostage too huh?" I unbuttoned her pants and slid them down with her panties.

"Damn, yo ass getting fat." I smacked it and trailed my tongue down her spine.

"I need a chair to take my time eating all this ass." My body was still healing but nothing stopped me from pleasing her. I grabbed the chair, put it behind her, made her bend down and touch her ankles.

"I swear I missed this." I used my hands to open her cheeks and stuck my face in her ass. I felt her hands grabbing my legs as she began experiencing the orgasm making her body tremble.

"Let me taste what I've missed C." I smacked her ass and her sweetness flooded my face. She tried to move but I held her there and finished having my snack. I turned her around and witnessed the same hunger for me in her eyes, that I had for her.

I laid her on the ground and allowed my fingers to dance around her pussy. She arched her back as I sucked on both nipples like a baby wanting his milk. I pushed two fingers inside, the pleasure drew and pushed through on my hand. I kissed up her body as she relaxed and once our eyes met, I knew she's the woman meant to be in my life.

"Don't cry C." I wiped her tears away.

215

"I can't help it. I love you so much Meek and I feel like I'm not good enough." I pressed my body against hers and thrusted inside. I stopped to allow her time to get used to me again. We had sex a lot and being without it for a few weeks will make it feel like the first time. I moved slowly in and out and felt her nails digging in my back.

"You're perfect for me C'Yani Bailey and I'm sorry for making you feel otherwise." Our lips met and just like old times she allowed me to make love to her in the office. It didn't matter how many times I watched her succumb to an orgasm, I still felt like she needed more.

"I love the shit outta you C." I moaned out staring at her suck my kids out. Not many women can get a man to cum this way but she had no problem.

****

"I'm scared Meek. What if she tempts you or any woman does for that matter?" I tied my sneaker and stood.

"I've never cheated on you and I won't. I apologize from the bottom of my heart for assuming you'd sleep with someone else and turned to another woman. You have no idea

216

how much it's fucking with me to see you hurting. I gave her something that belonged to you and fucked up in the process but know she will never be you. She'll never be first in my life and if you want me to make her lose the baby, I will."

"Meek."

"C'Yani, I don't know what you did to me but I'll do anything to see a smile on your face. I don't ever wanna witness the hate in your eyes you had for me again. It tore me up to hear you say those words because you are perfect."

"You're perfect for me too but you only get this one pass Meek. I can't go through the same thing." I smiled listening to her take me back. I don't care how corny it is. This woman had me strung out on her in every way possible.

"As far as your baby mama goes, I don't want any dealings with her. If that is your child then we'll deal with it but until then, she needs to stay away from me." I laughed at her tryna figure out a way to close the blouse I ripped.

"Here. Put this on."

"What are you going to wear?" I helped her put my shirt on.

"I'm good but ain't no way you're walking around with an open shirt." I pulled it down and it was almost to her knees.

"Come on." I grabbed her hand and opened the door.

"About time."

"Don't come for me Monica." C said and they started laughing. She tried to speak hood and it always sounded funny.

"Yo bitch, come here." I walked to the cubicle I saw Theresa sitting in.

"Meek, not here."

"Nah. I need to make it known to everyone in this motherfucker."

"It's ok." I ignored her because we both know it's not. She doesn't like confrontation or to be embarrassed.

"Theresa, we don't know if that's my kid and until we do, don't hit my line. Second..." I lifted her out the seat by the arm.

"If my girl comes home and tells me you're fucking with her, I promise to end you. Do I make myself clear?" She sucked her teeth.

"DO I?" She jumped and I think others did too.

"You smell that?"

"Smell what?" Theresa asked lifting her arms to see if it's her.

"That's my woman's pussy and ass all over my face."

"Really Meek?"

"Damn right really. You wanted to know why I never went down on you. Let me tell you why? This woman has the best pussy I've ever tasted. Why would I taint it with some community shit?"

"Whatever."

"Whatever my ass. I plan on walking around like this all the time so unless you wanna smell this good shit, stay the fuck out my face." I pushed her and heard all the women laugh as she hit the ground.

"My main man Meek."

"You know my boss?" I shook hands with Marcus.

"Hell Yea. We go way back to when I used to visit in the summer. He played ball with us and some other shit too."

"It's a small world." I heard C'Yani say.

219

"It is. Let me get your number so we can catch up." He handed it to me and walked with us down to her office.

"Can you put some clothes on and why does my best employee have a long T-shirt on?"

"I had to make up in her office and ripped her blouse."

"Oh my God Meek. Why would you tell him that?" Her face was flustered.

"Like I said, we cool like that."

"It's ok C'Yani. When my wife comes and the door is shut, we not talking." He laughed and went back to his office.

"It's fine babe. You leaving anyway." I held her against the door frame.

"I'll see you in my bed tonight?"

"I am not going to your house until your ex is found." I laughed because ain't nobody tell her shit but lil Faz. Him and Mystic are always over her house or Teri's. That's how tight they all became.

"I'll be in yours then." I kissed her lips and grabbed my stuff.

"But you don't know where I live."

"I know everything about my future." I pressed the elevator button.

"Let me know when that doctor's appointment is. If one of my kids fertilized those eggs, I wanna see too." I stepped on and stared at her mouth hit the floor. I don't know if she's pregnant but her titties grew, her ass got fatter and the pussy is wetter. In my eyes it can only mean she's pregnant.

"I love you C." It's like the entire office got quiet. Everyone stared at the two of us.

"I love you too babe." She blew me a kiss as the elevator door closed. How the hell did this corny ass woman get me to be lost in love?

I walked in my office when the elevator doors closed and felt a presence behind me. I said a prayer in my head before turning around asking God not to allow this woman to verbally or physically attack me. I'm sure once Meek embarrassed her she had a lot to say. Lucky for me, it was only Monica standing there with a smirk on her face.

"Before I sit, were you guys on this chair?" I didn't answer and offered her a seat. I cleaned everything off before leaving the office.

"I'm so glad he dug in her ass."

"You know I didn't want that." I never want to bring attention to myself. Especially; at the work place.

"Oh no. I couldn't tell." We both focused on the door Theresa leaned on.

"If I'm not mistaken, didn't her man just tell you not to say anything to her?" Monica stood and I asked her to relax.

"Let me guess. You fucking him too?"

"Are you crazy? I have a man."

"Anyway." She rolled her eyes at Monica.

222

"Ms. Bailey, I don't appreciate your man approaching me the way he did and putting hands on me."

"I have no idea what you're speaking of. Do you Monica?" Meek taught me a long time ago if a person you barely speak to questions you, don't answer because most likely you're being recorded.

"Nope and I been here all day."

"It's ok. The video footage will show everything." I rose to my feet and felt pain in between my legs. That's what I get for holding out.

"He does have a way of making you walk funny right?" She had a ton of sarcasm in her voice.

"What is it you want from me Theresa? Huh? I left him alone after catching you giving him oral sex in his truck." Monica sucked her teeth.

"However; as you can see he found me. If he wanted you in any shape or form, I think we both know he would've let it be known. So, I ask you again. What do you want from me?"

"When this child is born, I don't need you coming with him to spend time or calling his phone when he visits. I also know you'll never be his first baby mama because I am so even though you may have him. I'll have something you'll never get no matter how hard you try."

"And that is?"

"His first child. *BOOM!* Now run and tell that."

"Ok and that means what? He's not going to be with you or allow you to taste that big ass dick you're desperately seeking." I moved towards her.

"If you touch her Theresa, I'm gonna put my hands on you." Monica began taking her earrings out. She's been my secretary now for a few years and I loved her like my sister. We didn't hang out a lot because she has a daughter but I still looked at her the same.

"It's ok." I stopped in front of Theresa.

"It's women like you who constantly chase taken men, in hopes to get them to leave the woman who has their heart. I'm here to tell you, corny or not that man ain't going nowhere because I'm not allowing you or any other woman to take him.

224

Now if he leaves on his own that's different but we both know it's not gonna happen anytime soon. Therefore; you can toss out all these threats and throw tantrums but the fact remains that Mekhi Gibson isn't leaving me."

"Mekhi Gibson." I laughed.

"How are you supposedly having a baby by a man whose real name you don't even know?"

"I knew that. You threw me off because we use his street name." Monica and I looked at each other and busted out laughing.

"Theresa after next week you don't have to see me anymore. Until then, stay out of my face and office."

"I can't wait for Meek to show his true colors. I'm gonna be standing there with my baby laughing at your stupid ass."

"Yea well stupid or not, I'm going to continue enjoying the ride you stressing over."

BOOM! I slammed the door in her face.

"You ok?"

"What do you think she means by his true colors?"

"The same colors he showed her. C'Yani he'd never treat you that way and we both know it. Don't let what she said make you question your relationship." I nodded and gave her half a smile.

"A few more days and we're outta here." I blew my breath in the air and rested my head on the chair.

"I hope he's worth all this." I said to myself when my secretary stepped out.

****

"Are you gonna walk past me and not speak?" Some woman asked. I had no idea who she was.

"I'm sorry have we met?" I stared at the woman and still had no clue. She was pretty and appeared to be pregnant. Her stomach isn't out there but it's big.

"I want you to stop sleeping with my man."

"I think you have me confused with someone else. The man I'm with doesn't deal with anyone else besides me and before you ask, yes I'm sure." I was confident in my statement until she hit me with this other mess.

"Oh yea. If he's your man then how am I expecting?"

226

"Wait! Are we talking about the same guy?"

"Listen here sweetie." She moved closer to me.

"You think you know Meek but you have no fucking idea the type of man he is." Now I'm pissed because this is the second time a woman said these words to me.

"He told me all about your corny, non-sexual ass."

"Excuse me!"

"Yea we laughed about you being clueless in the bedroom." She looked me up and down.

"Meek is well endowed so I know you ain't fucking him right. Especially if he came to me."

"Who are you again?" My phone started ringing and it was Meek. I ignored it and he called right back. After sending him to voicemail two more times, I noticed a large man coming in my direction. The phone rang again and this time I answered.

"Hello." The woman glanced around and noticed the large man walking towards us.

"C'Yani when I call you need to answer." I could tell he was upset.

"Is everything ok?"

"I need you to back away slowly from her and pretend nothing's wrong." How did he know I was speaking to someone?

"Umm ok." I looked at the lady.

"I have to go." I turned to leave and felt the woman coming up.

"Walk faster babe. Please." I glanced around the mall wondering if he could see me.

"What's wrong?"

"C, that's Kim. I need you away from her. Someone is coming for you."

"Is it the large guy?"

"Large guy? No Faz is there. He saw her from the top floor."

"GET HER!" The woman yelled and I ran.

"Meek, they're chasing me."

"FUCKKKK! I'm almost there. C, I don't care what you have to do. Just keep running and don't stop. Cut in between cars if you have to."

"Oh my God."

"What C? What happened?"

"Her sister is standing in front of me."

"Smack that bitch. She's scary."

"Ummm."

"DO IT C'YANI." I lifted my foot and kicked her in the stomach.

"You bitch." She fell on the ground. I heard what sounded like fireworks and turned to see the large guy laid out on the ground.

"You ok?" Lil Faz walked to me and snatched the phone out my hand.

"Yea she good. We by Macy's." He hung up and my body was shaking. I couldn't calm down.

"Sit. He's almost here." He pointed to the bench and went to where the sister laid.

"You fucked up." He picked her up and told her if she moved, he'd shoot her in the back. Cops rolled up out of nowhere and the scene became chaotic.

"Take her outta here. Tell Shak not to do anything until the bitch tells where her sister is." I felt Meek pick me up and rested my head on his shoulder. *What a day?*

"You ok?" I sat C in my truck.

"Yea. Shaking up a bit though."

"I'm gonna go see what's up and be right back. Lock the doors."

"You think she'll return?"

"I'm not sure but she's probably watching. I'll be right here." I pointed to where the cops were.

"I can see you." I kissed her lips, closed the door and hit the alarm on it. If she got out or someone tried to get in, I'd hear it.

"Y'all know this dude?" The cop asked and both of us told him no.

"Let us handle this and Faz if we have any questions we'll contact you." The detective is friends with Shawn so we knew they wouldn't look into it any further. Especially; since he told him dude followed and chased C out the mall. I wanted to ask my cousin if he knew where Kim was but decided to wait. I don't want anyone getting rid of the bitch but me. We made plans to speak later because I wanted to get my girl home and find out what all happened.

I sat in my truck, turned the ignition and couldn't help but notice my girls' thighs. They were thicker than normal and regardless of her being on the pill, it's clear those shits ain't working. I smiled at the thought of her carrying my first child. I say first because I highly doubt that dumb bitch Theresa is pregnant by me.

Instead of going to her house, I drove to the ER and parked. She seemed to be confused and it's fine because I never mentioned why we came. We easily could've purchased a store test but then we'd have to wait for a doctor's appointment and all that. I do know if you come here and they find out you are, they automatically give you an ultrasound. At least this way we'll both see the baby sooner than later.

"My girl was almost attacked and she's shaken up a bit. She's also been experiencing a lot of vomiting and headaches."

"Meek!" I looked over at her and smirked.

"Anyway, it could be anxiety or something else."

"Is she pregnant?" The receptionist stared at C'Yani.

232

"No I'm not." She rushed to say.

"We don't know."

"Ok. Let me get some information and the nurse will come triage her before sending her in the back."

"Say what you want but it's obvious you wanna know too. Otherwise; you would've walked out." I told her and took a seat. She remained quiet the entire time, all the way up until the doctor returned with a machine and paperwork. He had her lie down and went through the results of the blood work, in which we found out she is indeed pregnant. My ass was souped, where her look was distant.

"Ok. Ms. Bailey you are exactly four weeks. Here's your baby and his or her heartbeat." He turned the machine up and I smiled. I couldn't believe I knocked her up and asked how it happened.

"I wasn't taking the pills the way I should've been. I kept forgetting because of everything I went through. Meek I'm not ready for a kid. What if...?" She stopped and the doctor stared at me.

"Doc, she was pregnant over a year ago and the baby was stillborn. How likely is it for history to repeat itself?"

"It's rare but it can happen. However; as long as her stress levels stay down, she eats and gets enough sleep. I don't see it happening again. If I may ask, what did you do during the last pregnancy? Was it healthy?"

"Yes. I mean the father had me stressing a lot, I wasn't eating or taking care of myself. The week before losing him, I had an appointment that went fine. I don't how I lost him." She broke down crying. I asked the doctor to give us a minute.

"I'm not him C'Yani. Trust that this baby will make it."

"How can you be sure? I mean everything was perfect until the end." I made her look at me.

"Because I'm gonna make sure you're happy at all times. My grandmother is gonna be fucking ecstatic and so is your mom. They're gonna bombard your life so much you'll ask me to make them stay away. Ma, this baby is a blessing and I'm happy as hell you're gonna be the mother."

"But you have another..." I cut her off.

"Even if I were the father, it's never gonna stop me from loving you or our child. I'm with you and only you."

"What if...?"

"No more what ifs. Let's enjoy this moment and find out the next step." I invited the doctor in and let him go over the discharge instructions. He also told her not to stress over what happened because it will make things worse and she could miscarry.

After leaving and stopping by the pharmacy to get the pills and food, I took her to my grandparents. She used to hate coming here but now that she gets in my grandfather's ass when he's inappropriate, it's not a problem. Plus, my grandmother wants to see her.

I sent a group message out to everyone the way Shak did but I also told them to let her mention it. She's still nervous and scared after what happened previously and to be honest, I am too. I won't leave her the way that nigga did but I want my child to make it.

****

235

"What's going on sexy lady?" My grandfather started up instantly.

"Move. I'm here to see nana." That's what my grandmother told C to call her.

"She don't wanna see yo ass."

"Did you just curse?"

"I'm gonna tell you like I tell everyone. I wasn't always saved and God uses ass in the Bible. I think." He put his finger under his chin like he really had to think about it.

"How in the hell did you become a reverend?" She rolled her eyes and went to find my grandmother.

"Hey son." My pops strolled in the living room slowly. After all this time, he's still recovering from the shit my ex did. I'm glad he was awake because I've been meaning to talk to him.

"I need to speak to you." He gave me a weird look and so did my grandfather. We walked out the back and sat on the deck. I needed a smoke.

"Everything ok?"

"I'm gonna kill Kim?" I lit the blunt.

236

"I expected it but why are you telling me?"

"You can't be that dumb son." My grandfather laughed.

"He's telling you because the devil has your spawn inside her." I told them how she broke in the house saying on video how he got her pregnant and she wants to tell people the baby is mine. He refuses to acknowledge the sexual act altogether. In his mind it never happened but those stab wounds and the fact she took the dick says different.

"That ain't my kid."

"It may not be but I'm telling you because she is indeed pregnant and the kid will die with her."

"It's not my kid so do what you have to." He walked in the house and slammed the door. My grandfather sat next to me.

"You do know that's your brother or sister in her stomach. Wait! That's your kid."

"Stop with the jokes." He knew when I wasn't playing and put his hands up in surrender. He's right but the less I thought about it, the easier it is to take her life. I'm happy my

237

father don't care because I would've hated to let her live until delivery.

"Do what you have to. Just don't mention it to him because he feels bad enough she caught him out there like that." I nodded and asked him to give me alone time. I continued smoking the blunt and laid my head back. *Where the fuck is this bitch hiding?"*

"You need to check on your man." Meek's grandfather said barging in the kitchen where me and his wife sat.

"What happened to him?" Panic set in as I thought about how angry he could get over certain things. If he's upset, something definitely went down.

I went to the screen that led to the back porch and stared at Meek. He seemed to be in a zone and I hated to bother him. I'm sure he won't mind and even though he would never hurt me, I'm always mindful of his attitude. I also don't want to piss him off more than he is.

I opened the door and made my way to where he was. Once he felt my presence, he looked up and instantly put the blunt down. He smiled, lifted my shirt to kiss my belly and placed me on his lap. I loved everything about this man and secretly prayed this is his first and only child. I would never wish death on another woman or for her to lose a child, so in my head the results will come back that he's not the father.

"I'm good ma."

"I didn't say anything."

239

"You don't have to. Once my grandfather went in and you came out, I knew he told you to check on me."

"You think you know everything."

"I'm wrong?"

"Not the point but you don't have to brag."

"Ain't nobody bragging sexy but I do know my family and you."

"You don't know me." I stood and so did he. His body pressed against mine as he placed his hand on the house and towered over me.

"I know you're a smart and caring woman. I know you're about to blow up when your business opens and I also know you strung me the fuck out." I covered my mouth.

"Regardless of being clueless sexually, once you learned, my ass been stuck. And that mouth is serious." I let my arms go around his neck.

"I've been strung out on you since the first nut." He couldn't stop laughing. I really did try and be hood for him but it never sounds right coming out.

"I think we need to go home because..." He cut me off.

"Home? I like the way those words sound."

"Yea well, I mean my home because I won't step foot in that other house until she's found and I mean it."

"It's all good. As long as I'm with you, home is wherever you are." He grabbed my hand and led us inside.

"We out." He kissed his grandparents and I noticed his father staring into space. He called me in the room. I let Meek's hand go and went to him.

"You ok?" He held both of my hands and the stare he gave was chilling. I mean goosebumps popped up on my arm and I felt nervous. Whatever he's about to say must be bad.

"My son is in love with you C'Yani."

"I'm in love with him too."

"Good because he's about to do something and I need you to be ok with it because I am."

"Huh?"

"He'll tell you when the time is right. Then again, he may not but just know it has to be done."

"Ok."

"Whatever you do, don't get mad or harbor any hate towards him."

"You're scaring me. Is it dangerous? Will he survive?"

"It's not so much dangerous as it is something that's unavoidable." I nodded but deep down I was scared.

"He won't let anything happen to you."

"Pops, don't be tryna kick it to my future."

"Never. She's too young for me. I wouldn't be able to hang." He winked and we all laughed. However; I still wanted to know what the hell is going on. I guess the best time to ask is when we get home.

****

"I probably got you pregnant again." Meek laughed and laid me on top of him. I listened to his heartbeat and swore ours was in sync.

"Meek."

"Yea babe."

"Why were you upset earlier?" He moved me off and had me lay on my side to look at him.

"Promise you won't get mad or upset.

242

"Is it that bad?"

"If I'm looking from your angle, then yes." I didn't know what to say.

"Promise me."

"Ok. I'm only making a promise because whatever it is must benefit all of you in the long run."

"And you."

"Me?"

"Yes you." He pulled me in closer and rested his hand on the small of my back.

"I'm going to kill Kim."

"Ok." I had no problem with it.

"Wait! She's pregnant."

"I know." He rolled on his back and used his arm to cover his face.

"Meek, I'm not ok with that."

"Look at it as she's having an abortion." I sat up and put my knees to my chest. After losing my child the way I did, I never want a woman to feel that way.

"My father isn't claiming the child and even if I didn't kill her, none of us would be bothered with the kid."

"But it's your brother or sister."

"NO IT'S NOT!" He yelled and I jumped.

"She basically raped my father and is now having an unwanted child. I understand why you'd be upset but if the situation was reversed and my father raped her, she wouldn't keep the child and probably ask someone to kill him."

"Meek, I don't..."

"This is why I didn't wanna tell you." He stood up and began putting his clothes on.

"You're leaving?"

"Yea because this conversation is bound to go left and I don't want you stressing."

"Too late." He walked over to my side and had me look at him. He continued getting dressed.

"Put some clothes on."

"For?"

"JUST DO IT!" He barked and like the scaredy cat I am, I rushed to get dressed. I saw him placing some of my things in a small bag along with my laptop and other stuff.

"What are you doing?"

"You done?" I grabbed my keys and phone.

"Yes." We walked downstairs and out the door in silence. He started his truck and pulled off. I badly wanted to ask where he was taking me but decided against it. He yelled at me twice already and I didn't want him to do it again. I stared out the window the entire ride and looked at him when we pulled up at my parents.

"Get out."

"Why are we here?" He gave me no response and grabbed my things. The front door opened and my mom had a huge grin on her face.

"What am I going to do with two grand babies at once?" I knew Meek sent a group text out about the pregnancy but didn't know he added my parents.

"Two?"

"If you spoke to your sister, you'd know." I sucked my teeth.

"Don't suck your teeth at me missy. You're not too old for me to pop you in your mouth."

"Sorry mommy. Meek why am I here?"

"Can you give us a minute?" She nodded and walked away from the door.

"You're gonna stay here until I find Kim."

"Meek, I'm a grown woman and..."

"I don't care what you are. You heard what the fuck I said."

"Don't speak to me like that."

"Then start listening C. My ex is out in the streets and no one knows where she is. I tell you I'm gonna find and kill her and you're not ok with it. However, what you're not gonna do is make me feel bad or lose my kid."

"I'm not trying to make you feel bad."

"I know you're not doing it purposely but your facial expression and the way you disapprove lets me know you don't want me to do it. C'Yani." He pulled me closer.

246

"You have no idea how scared I was to know she found you at the mall and almost took you away. My heart was beating a mile a minute and even though we were on the phone, I had no clue of the danger you were in."

"But I want to stay with you. Meek, I won't say anything. I'll even stay at your place."

"I know you're safe here and your parents are gonna make sure you eat and take good care of our baby."

"Meek."

"Your parents said I can stay anytime I want ma. Don't make this harder than it has to be."

"Hold up. Did you plan this?" He blew his breath in the air.

"I had to C. It's the only way for me to keep sane when I'm on these streets looking for her."

"You don't love me."

"WHAT?" The anger was evident in his voice.

"If you loved me, I'd be up under you and..." He lips pressed against mine.

"Nice try ma." He pulled away and smirked.

"You know and feel how much I love you. This reverse psychology isn't gonna work on me." I folded my arms and pouted. I hated that he always knew what I'm gonna do or say before I do it.

"I only brought you here tonight because after hearing how upset you were over the situation, I don't wanna get upset and take it out on you."

"I'm fine Meek."

"I know you are." His hands roamed my body.

"I'm gonna pick you up in the morning for breakfast."

"I'm not going." I tried to storm off and he caught me.

"C'Yani don't make me take you to my truck and give you some act right." I gave him a devious grin.

"Oh yea." We went to the truck and did nasty things to each other. By the time we finished it was after two in the morning.

"Have your ass ready at seven."

"Meek, that's too early."

"Too bad. You shouldn't have hopped on this dick."

"I'll hop on that good dick anywhere." He snatched me by the head and stuck his tongue down my throat.

"I love you C and I'll see you in a few hours."

"Ok babe."

"C, I'm doing what's best for you and my baby."

"I know you are and I'm excited." I smiled and rubbed my stomach.

"I love you Meek. Be careful." I went to the door and closed it. I stared at him pull off out the window and heard my phone ring.

"Yes Meek."

"Go to bed."

"I am." We said I love you again and hung up. I hopped in the shower and went straight to sleep. I hope he finds Kim soon because I want to lay up under him.

"I'm here to see Mrs. Samuel." I told the bitch at the front desk.

"She's busy right now. I can set you up with an appointment for..." she glanced at the computer I guess to find an available date.

"That won't be necessary." Shak and I moved past her. I went back to her and snatched the phone out her hand.

"It wouldn't be wise for you to contact the police when we both know she's either on her knees or getting fucked." I put the phone on the receiver and smirked.

"You ready to do this?" Shak asked and I think he was more ready than I was.

"Let's do this." Both of us stepped on the elevator and went to the next floor up. Evidently the bitch had her own private office. The doors opened and we walked off and down the hall.

"Faz said he left the door unlocked." I nodded and turned the knob quietly. If the shit was gonna work we couldn't make a sound. We were gonna use a different person for this plan but he loved fucking with older chicks.

"Oh shit Fazza. I'm about to cum again. Yessssss." The woman screamed out as my little cousin fucked the shit outta the district attorney. He had her on all fours on the ground. His ass was still fully dressed, while she had nothing on.

"Hurry the fuck up. I got shit to do and I need you to suck this nut out." Shak and I stood quietly looking down at our phone. Neither of us wanted to watch but the pictures were gonna be perfect.

See we couldn't figure out a way to get Jasmine without having to deal with the media due to how powerful her mom is. Therefore; we had to come up with a plan to get her in an uncompromising position. Who knew she was a ho like her daughter? And we found that out from one of the chicks Faz mess with.

She's a paralegal for Mrs. Samuel and mentioned that this woman has sex in her office all the time. No one says anything because they don't wanna jeopardize their jobs. It's all good because it came in handy for us.

251

What made it even better, is the fact she loved fucking young hood dudes. It wasn't easy getting her to mess with my cousin and she had a lot of doubts. He had to basically treat her like his woman. She had him bring her food to the job, meet at certain locations in other towns and would text him all through the night. A few times she had Face Timed him for phone sex with her husband in the other room. No wonder Jasmine has no problem coming for taken men. The apple don't fall far from the tree. I'm not saying my cousin is taken but she sure the hell is.

"Suck all this dick." Shak and I turned around. We do not wanna see his shit. Any of those pics, he can take himself.

"Oh shit. This bitch got a photo with Obama." Shak yelled and snatched the picture off the shelf.

"OH MY GOD! WHO ARE YOU AND HOW DID YOU GET IN HERE?"

"Bitch how you asking questions with cum in your hair and on the side of your mouth?" Shak turned around and busted out laughing while Faz continued to pull his jeans up.

"Excuse me!" She attempted to cover her body but it was no use. It was nice and you could see the muscles from working out.

"There's no excuse for cheating on your husband." I walked over, grabbed her by the head and made her stand.

"What do you want?" She was shaking and Faz kept smacking her ass. Talking about he needs to see it jiggle more.

"Your daughter is causing a lotta problems."

"Which one?"

"Jasmine. We know the other one ain't doing shit. Oh but you know that since you're fucking her husband too. How's your son in law dick feel?"

"You foul as shit for that. How you think she'll take it when she finds out?" Shak asked.

"Please don't tell. What do you need me to do?"

"Why don't you want her to know?" Shak kept questioning her. I was curious myself because she pretends not to care.

"She has a lotta health issues and it's the reason he cheats."

"Makes no sense and put some clothes on." I pushed her to the ground and smiled thinking about when I did it to C'Yani. The only difference is, I wanted her and she tried to play me.

"She's a heavy drinker and one of her kidneys failed. She goes to dialysis a few times a week and hasn't given him sex. He came to me and asked if I'd sleep with him to keep him from leaving her."

"Say what?" Me and Shak said at the same time Faz walked out the bathroom.

"I don't want my daughter to grow old alone so I give him pussy when he wants. It's not hurting anyone because no one knows."

"They do now." Shak replayed the entire conversation and her eyes got big.

"This and the photos will damage your career along with you allowing niggas to walk you've been sleeping with." She fell back in her chair.

"What do you need?"

"I'm going to kill your daughter, so when it happens play the distraught mother and all that but if for one second I think you're on other shit, everything will be revealed and you'll be next. Are we clear?"

"Wait! I'm not ok with you coming in here telling me you're about to murder my child."

"And I'm not ok with her fucking with my girl every chance she gets. I've told her repeatedly to leave her alone but she don't listen." I shrugged my shoulders.

"And the bitch watched me fuck her best friend. Where they do that at?"

"Teri?"

"Yea Teri."

"Who's the chick you're with?"

"Teri sister." She covered her mouth and the expression on her face let me know she's about to reveal some foul shit.

"What?"

"Please tell me she's not the woman Jasmine and Mia attacked in the hotel room." I ran up on her and snatched her out the chair.

"They came by my house talking about some woman they beat up really bad and then Jasmine made a video having sex with some guy to make it look like the girl." You have no idea how mad I was.

"Where is she?"

"I'm not telling you."

"Oh, but you are?"

BAM! I slammed her face against the desk but not hard enough to break her nose.

"Where the fuck is she?" The bitch still didn't answer so I lifted her out the seat and literally threw her across the room. My foot connected with her stomach. My cousins had to pull me off because I was about to kill her. I put the gun to her head.

"You don't have to tell me because I'm gonna find her. Start prepping for the funeral." I was getting ready to hit her over the head with the butt of my gun.

"Meek." I heard my girls voice and turned around. Faz must've called and put her on the phone.

"Yea babe." I snatched the phone out his hand and gave him a death stare. Why in the hell did he call her?

"Are you ok?"

"I'm good. Where you at?"

"Getting ready for the grand opening. You're still coming as my date right?"

"Ain't no other nigga escorting you nowhere." She started laughing.

"I can't wait to show you off. Oh, and I think we need to christen my office." I grabbed my dick. C knew how to turn me on.

"Hell yea we do. I'm gonna have that juicy ass bent over the desk and..."

"Bro we don't wanna hear that shit. Let's get outta here." Faz shouted and continued rolling up at the desk. He don't care where he smoke at.

"A'ight C. I'll be there soon."

"I love you Meek and whatever you're doing be careful so you can come home to us." I smiled as she referred to us. She was nervous at first about the pregnancy but now she's very excited. It's the exact reason I have her staying with her parents unless I pick her up. I know they won't let anything happen to her and all of us want this baby to make it. Honestly, I see her having a breakdown if it doesn't and I'm not about to let that happen.

"Love you too ma." I hung up and handed the phone back to Faz.

"What we doing about this bitch?" Shak stood in front of her.

"Yo bitch, get up." She nodded and began holding on to the chair to try and stand. I gave zero fucks on how bad she looked. Blood was coming down her head and her lip was busted. She probably has some internal bleeding too but who cares?

"Remember what the fuck I said."

"Please don't kill Jasmine. Let me talk to her." I chuckled.

"I may have allowed it had you not mentioned her being the one who attacked my girl."

"Please!" She begged and the three of us walked out.

"What you think she's gonna do?" Shak pressed the button on the elevator.

"Call her daughter and ask what's going on. All it will do is bring her out and I'll be waiting."

"It's time you tell C'Yani."

"I know."

"Regardless of Jasmine missing, something tells me she's going to find a way to tell C."

"Why don't you want her to know anyway?" Faz asked and blew smoke in the air. Yea, he lit the blunt on the elevator.

"I didn't want her to feel as if Jasmine could get me in bed again. You know women think shit like that. And it's in the past, they're not friends and I don't see the reason why. But with a bitch like Jasmine I'm sure she'll make it more than it is."

"You know it." Shak said and we all stepped off.

"Have a good day gentleman." Faz friend said and smiled.

"I'm gonna call you tonight." She blushed like a high school girl and we looked at him.

"What? She has some fire between her legs." We waved him off and hopped in the truck. Now I have to find Kim's stupid ass.

Jasmine

Today I'm supposed to drop by my parents' house for dinner. I have no idea why my mother even wants this when none of us seen each other in months. It's not that I don't wanna go, its more or less of why she wants us there. My mom is very distant to all of her kids. We don't have the family dinners, talks or even vacations so this is not going to go well.

I finished putting my clothes on and walked over to Ty lying in bed asleep. I had to move a few towns over because I'm not sure what Meek or Shak will do if they run into me. I don't think Meek found out about us attacking C'Yani but then again, Kim told me they kidnapped her sister from the mall. I told those two idiots tryna grab C'Yani in a public place wouldn't work because most likely someone would be watching. The best spot to get her would've been at work but that's impossible now because she's about to open the new building. Meek has security out the ass there for her.

Anyway, I haven't really been in town and don't need to be at this point. Teri whooped my ass and her man damn near killed me. I don't know what he was upset over. Shit, I was only watching and got myself off. I can say he's working with something and the way he fucked Teri had a bitch in heat. I didn't mean to be as loud as I was but he was doing the damn thing.

I'm mad as hell she got him first because word on the street now is, he moved her in that big ass house he has. Ty lives comfortably but he corny and I want a Shak or Meek too. Hell, I would've even taken the younger cousin with the funny eyes but he had a serious attitude problem.

"Where you going?" Ty wrapped his arms around my waist and kissed my neck.

"To my parents' house." He looked at me in the mirror.

"You think that's a good idea?"

"Why wouldn't it be?" He swung me around to face him. I stared in his eyes and had no doubt in my mind that he's in love with me.

"You said, the thugs are angry with you. What if they see you go in?"

"Awww you're worried." I smiled and pecked his lips.

"Jasmine regardless of how we got together, I do love you."

"I love you too babe." I turned back around and continued putting my makeup on.

Ty is a good guy, minus the fact he cheated on his precious C'Yani but I truly believe if she had been a better woman in the bedroom, no one would've been able to get next to him. He may have cheated on a drunk night and he did deny a lot of my requests in the beginning.

It took me showing up at one of his parents stores to get his attention. We sat it the car talking, I bent down, gave him head and the rest is history. I don't think he'll dip out on me because like I said before, he gets whatever he wants from me sexually. I mean what would be the purpose?

"I'll see you later babe and I promise to be safe." I kissed him again and headed out the door.

On the drive over, I thought about how sick my sisters been lately and couldn't help but wonder if her husband is still cheating. Of course, I slept with him. He kept saying he was gonna leave her and knowing how much she loved him, I didn't want that for her. Plus, he needed to take care of her. Sickness and health are what the vows say but some can't stay around when the spouse gets as bad as my sister.

The dialysis was taken a toll on her from what he told me. I asked why he's cheating with her sister and he said, it's because we look alike and she's who he thinks of. I could get offended but what for? Call me what you want, but it's for my sister and I rather it be with me than some random off the streets.

I pulled in my parents' driveway and hurried to get inside. I could smell the food as soon as I walked in. My father was in the living room watching television as always. My niece and nephew were running around and my fake ass brother in law had my sister on his lap. I could tell from the outside looking in, he's still in love with my sister. But like most men, his dick has to be satisfied and because of it; sent him elsewhere. I strolled in the kitchen and found my mother whispering on the phone. She must've felt my presence and turned around.

"I'll call you back." She hung up and outta nowhere her hand connected to my face so hard, I stumbled back a little.

"What the fuck?" I rubbed my face and became nervous when my mother stepped closer to me.

"How dare you put me in a position like this?" She started raining more blows on me. My father and sisters husband Rick, had to pull her off. I can fight, but I'd never swing on her.

"Ma, what's going on?" I heard my sisters voice and it wasn't until that moment, I realized how much healthier she looked. Her skin wasn't pale, she had more body weight and her hair and nails were done. I didn't pay attention when I walked by in the beginning because my brother in law was feeling all over her like a pervert.

"Your sister here, has been causing ruckus in other people's relationships."

"What are you talking about?" I stared at Rick who had no reaction. There's no way she knows about us.

"You watched your best friend have sex with her man and the woman you attacked, is the girlfriend of a man who wants you dead. Actually, both of them are gunning for you."

My sister handed me some tissue to wipe my nose. How the hell did she know this?

"Let me explain."

"Explain what Jasmine. I thought you and mom were only sleeping with my husband. Who knew you were messing with other people." Both me and my mother's mouth hit the floor. My father walked in at the end of her statement and you could see the look of confusion on his face.

"Hold on. You knew?" My sister had her arms folded.

"Yes, and I was gonna save this conversation for after dinner but why wait? I do wanna know how either of you were ok with it?"

"How we're ok with it? You seem to be ok handling the news."

"Did you ever ask your sister why she drank the way she did?" Rich finally spoke up. None of us said a word.

"Your sister cheated on me a lot and gave me a disease. Unbeknownst to all of you, we were separated for a while.

Hurt and alone, I slept with both of you and made you believe it's because she wouldn't have sex with me."

"WHAT?" My sister had a few tears coming down her face.

"I knew she'd hurt the way I did, if I had sex with someone in her family. She had to see not only could I do it too, but I wanted the pain to be ten times worse than what she inflicted on me."

"I'm sorry sis." I tried to hug her but she backed up.

"I only came to this dinner to let you two whores know, my husband and I went to counseling and we're gonna stay together."

"Whore?"

"Yes whore. Regardless of what he did, neither of you even thought about my feelings. Neither of you once said, this isn't right and continued sleeping with him like I wasn't the sister or daughter who almost died."

"Sis, I thought he would leave you and..."

"FUCK THAT! YOU SHOULD'VE NEVER ALLOWED IT TO HAPPEN." She began getting upset and I noticed Rick take her hand in his.

"How are you even better?" I asked wanting to know why she looked better.

"It just so happened that my husband was the perfect match for my kidney and gave me his. So you see, regardless of the affair you two had with him, he's never gonna leave his wife."

"Ok, so he gave you a kidney, you gave him a disease, now what? Y'all about to live happily ever after." My sister stood in front of me.

"You damn right we are." She punched me in my face and kept hitting me. Once Rick pulled her off, she swung on my mom and the two of them went at it.

"How you fighting us and he's the one who cheated?" She smirked and lifted his shirt. There was a humongous scar on his side.

"What the hell is that?"

"The night he told me about y'all, I stabbed him with a screwdriver all the way down. He needed over a hundred stitches and a blood transfusion." She let his shirt down.

"I knew he'd get me back but never in a million years did I think, it would be with my own sister and mother." She wiped the few tears rolling down her face and told the kids to get their things ready.

"I hate y'all and never wanna see you again."

"So you'll forgive him and not us?"

"Yes and you know why?" He held her back.

"Because not only did he give me a kidney, he wasn't my fucking sister or mother. All of you knew better and instead of rejecting his advances, you went with it. One of you could've called and told me. But no. You're both sluts and I pray karma gets both of you." She stormed out the kitchen and all of us followed. I went to grab my things and saw my father coming down the steps with two luggage's.

"Where are you going?" My mother asked.

"I forgave you for cheating last year and you swore it was once and wouldn't happen again." Damn, I had no idea my mother was doing it like that.

"I didn't cheat with anyone else." The doorbell rang and Rick went to answer it.

"You're a fucking liar. I may not have said anything but over the last few weeks, you've been staying at work late again and up all night on the phone." I covered my mouth because I always thought they had the perfect relationship.

"YOOOO!" We heard Rick shout and saw him walking towards us backwards. None of us knew why, until we saw a shotgun pointed at him. The guys had masks on and were dressed on black.

"We're here for Jasmine." The voice said.

"What the hell are you doing in my house?" My mom shouted and in walked a nightmare.

"Bitch, I fucked you in here a few times. Now where the fuck is your daughter?" He turned to everyone and stopped when his eyes met mine. *This nigga is really about to kill me.*

"You look beautiful C." Meek said standing behind me as I placed the diamond studs in my ear.

I had on a long, black, strapless dress he brought. The split only came to my knee because he said any higher up and men would fantasize about what's his. My hair flowed down my back and my makeup is always on point. I didn't wear a lot but enough to know it's there.

The Giuseppe shoes just came out he said I had to have them. There's no way his woman would look a mess, especially; on my big night. I swear he's everything I wanted in a man. Too bad I didn't meet him first and spent those years and wasted tears with Ty.

Tonight, is my grand opening and I couldn't be happier. I had a few food vendors, a small boutique and even a convenient store in my building. I still allowed Teri to have free range of the floor she occupied because she's still my sister. Plus, my mom told me she wouldn't allow Jasmine to work here. I guess she realized the woman is making her lose.

Meek told me how she watched my sister and Shak have sex. He also told me Teri whooped her ass over saying she wanted him. At least she started to see the hateful things her so called friend was doing. Granted, it took forever but when you don't want certain things to be true, denial can be your best friend.

"Thanks babe and you have no idea how much seeing you in this suit is turning me on."

"That's the purpose." He kissed my neck and handed me a velvet box.

"What's this for?"

"I'm proud of you C."

"You pushed me to have my own so I should be buying you something." I went to my top drawer and handed him a small velvet box too.

"It's a token of my appreciation." He opened it and grinned.

"Damn ma. These are fire." I brought him a pair of six carat diamond studs. He looked sexy as hell when he wore the smaller ones he had. I'm sure he could afford to purchase bigger ones but I wanted to do something nice for him.

"Open yours." He watched as my eyes grew.

"Meek this is too much." I gasped at the diamond necklace that looked like a tennis bracelet. It was shining bright and I couldn't help but wonder how much it cost.

"Lift your hair up ma." I turned, lifted my hair and smiled in the mirror as he put it on. I felt like Julia Roberts in pretty woman. The necklace isn't the same but still.

"How do I look?"

"Gorgeous."

"Let's get out of here before I lift this dress up." I told him and his hands went to my side.

"I wanna save this for afterwards." I grabbed my clutch and phone.

"For?"

"I want you to make me moan in one of the bathrooms."

"What?" He laughed and held my hands going down the steps. We got dressed here because Teri was at my parents.

I had no words for her. I'm not being childish and I'm not holding grudges. I just refuse to deal with any nonsense right now.

"You know how people have spontaneous sex in the weirdest places?"

"Yea."

"I want to do that."

"Ma, we've Christened your office plenty of times already."

"Exactly but not with over 150 people there."

"Ok but you're a screamer so expect them to know what I'm doing."

"Whatever." He opened the door and my mouth dropped.

"A Rolls Royce limo Meek?"

"You're a BOSS ma. You have to show out."

"This is too much." He walked me to the car and the driver stepped out to open the door.

"Babe." I allowed some tears to fall looking at the flowers and bags inside.

"You deserve everything I'm gonna give you." We sat and he had me open all the bags.

There were business cards, pens with the company name, a new Apple laptop, and a business phone. He didn't want anyone having my personal number. Another bag held a Celine Purse and wallet to match. The Louboutin bag held two pair of shoes and a purse. By the time I finished looking through them all, we were pulling up. The local media and a few news stations were there, thanks to the mayor Meek is friends with.

"Go do your thing ma." The driver opened the door and I felt like someone was watching me.

"What's wrong?"

"Security is tight right?"

"Hell yea. Even if I didn't hire anyone the mayor is here with a ton of other politicians. They have their own as well.

"I'm gonna be next to you all night. If by some chance I need the bathroom you know all my family is here." I nodded and stepped out. I heard someone mention my name and the media came over full force. Cameras and recorders were all in my face. I turned to see Meek smiling and talking to his rude ass cousin Fazza. I continued talking and made sure to keep Meek in my vision. There were a ton of beautiful women in attendance and I refused to let them smile in his face.

Throughout the night, people came upstairs to congratulate me and even spoke to Monica about setting up appointments. I noticed my sister speaking to potential clients and felt like everything was going fine. The vendors were even making money.

"Can I have your attention?" I turned and saw my man on stage.

"C'Yani, come up here." I loved the stern voice and even though people may have thought he was being rude, I didn't. I stepped up and looked in the crowd to see he had everyone's attention.

"First off, congratulations on this being such a huge success. It's perfect, just like you."

"Babe, I'm not perfect."

"You're perfect for me, which is why I chose you to spend the rest of my life with." He got down on one knee and I almost passed out. Ty proposed but for some reason this one shocked me. Yes, we've been together for a year and some change, off and on but never in a million years did I think he'd want to settle down with me.

"C'Yani Bailey, you're corny, smart, beautiful, make your own money and have me wrapped around your finger. In a million years, I never thought I'd meet someone as perfect. My heart doesn't even beat right when you're away. You're like my legs, and I can't walk around without you. C, there's no other woman I wanna grow old with. I love you in every kinda way possible. Will you marry me?" I had so many tears falling down my face nothing I did could make them stop.

"Well? Is your white ass gonna marry my cousin or not?" I rolled my eyes and watched Ty smack him upside the head.

"Of course, I'll marry you babe." He slid the huge yellow diamond on my finger. I heard women saying, *Damn* and *I want a man like him*. He stood and both of us couldn't wait for our mouths to connect. The crowd erupted in claps and cheers.

"That bitch looks like she can't fuck. She's the type to think being a freak is nasty." I heard Meek's voice over the loud speaker. Yet; he's standing here holding my hand.

"C'Yani was clueless as fuck in the bedroom. She didn't know how to suck my dick or ride me."

"Yo, What the fuck?" Meek barked and I saw people whispering.

"Meek, what's going on?"

"I don't know."

"That bitch looks like she can't fuck. She's the type to think being a freak is nasty. C'Yani was clueless as fuck in the bedroom. She couldn't suck dick or ride me." Those words repeated themselves again. I saw Shak run up on stage along with big Faz, Mazza and Mystic. Each of them were looking for something.

"How you turn this loud speaker off?" Mystic asked and I pointed to the screen.

"Oh shit."

278

"Meek, that's not gonna fit in my coochie. It's too big."
You saw me jump off the desk in his office and get my clothes off the floor. I glanced around the room and people were leaving and some were shaking their heads.

"Good evening everyone." Meek froze when he heard the voice.

"I want to say a few things before you leave the vicinity."

"Ma, I need to know how to shut this off." Meek was standing in front of me trying to figure out what to say. He knew this was unacceptable.

"It's set up in the security room." He wiped my eyes and I looked down at my ring. He told Mystic and Shak where to go since they've been here before.

"I'll break your fucking neck if you even think about taking that ring off." He said it in a tone I've never heard him speak to me in.

"Meek, you said all those bad things about me. How could you?" I could tell he wanted to answer but she spoke again.

"This public service announcement is brought to you by Jasmine Samuel who is the district attorneys' daughter. She's been sleeping with Ms. Bailey's boyfriend for years now." I stared at Teri who had a shocked look on her face. I couldn't tell if it's because someone told or she really had no clue.

"Oh, she's slept with Mr. Meek as well." I had to be hearing things because there's no way she just said that. Meek ran his hand over his head staring at me. His silence let me know it's true and before I could ask questions she continued.

"Also Mr. Meek. Our baby is due in a few months so I suggest you get prepared."

"Why isn't this shit off yet?"

"One more thing." No one said a word as my parents and some of Meek's family came towards us.

"Direct your eyes back to the screen." Everyone's head turned and there was a photo of Theresa, his other baby mother.

"C'Yani, Meek will never ever change." Another video popped up of Theresa giving him head. Ten seconds later the show was over because the screen went black and the sound was gone.

"I'm gonna get her C."

"WHEN MEEK? HUH?" I was not only hurt but embarrassed and humiliated. He was supposed to make sure this night was perfect and his crazy ex ruined it all.

"This is the biggest night of my life and once again your baggage made a mess out of it. I can't do this." I went to step off the stage and felt him grip my arm.

"I know you're mad but I'm gonna remind you one more time in case I wasn't clear the first time."

"Meek let her arm go." Zia tried to pull his hand off my elbow.

"If you take that motherfucking ring off, I'm gonna do more than break your neck. Now fuck with me if you want."

"MEEK!" His grandmother yelled and it took Shak pushing him away to get off me. I ran off the stage and out the door to take me toward the stairs. How could this happen? How could she get into the system and do this? I had so many questions and no answers. I sat on the steps, grabbed my stomach and cried my eyes out.

"I think that went well, don't you?" I looked up and saw his ex-Kim standing in front of me with some guy. Maybe I shouldn't have run off because this isn't going to end well.

I stood there in shock as Meek's ex played that audio and video footage. When her voice first came on, I had no idea who she was but Shakim must've because he took off toward the stage. All the guys were trying their hardest to find out how to shut it off. Usually you'd just pull the cord out the wall but the way my sister had it set up, you had to go in the security room to do it. She wanted to make sure people couldn't interfere with anything. However; someone did and now the whole room is in total chaos.

I had Monica take the Mayor, other politicians and anyone we could move fast out and give them a tour. They heard a little of what was said but we got them out before the video played. Others stayed to be nosy but we eventually got them out too. The only people in here now is our families. Meek is going off because he knows like I do, that this will trump the proposal and C'Yani will walk away.

I would never wish this type of embarrassment on anyone; including my sister. We may not be speaking but this shit is fucked up on so many levels. The thing I don't understand is, how did someone even get the footage? The part about C'Yani saying he's too endowed for her happened in his office and the rest is probably before they got together and right after. I'd be mad too but he can't control what went down. Shakim taught me that a long time ago when his ex tried to kill me.

"Teri go find your sister and take her to your mom's."

"Babe, you know she hates me."

"I know but she needs you. Plus, I want you outta here too. This bitch is lurking somewhere and it's no telling what she has up here sleeve."

"Ok. Which way did she go?"

"Towards the stairs. Take one of the security dudes with you and call me when y'all are in route to the house. Love you." He pressed his lips on mine and walked back over to Meek and the guys. I felt someone staring and turned to see his mom giving me the evil eye. This woman had to be the most miserable person I ever met.

"Are you going to find your sister?" My dad asked.

"Yea. Shakim wants me to bring her to your house and wait for him there."

"Ok. We'll wait for you two in the car." I kissed both of them on the cheek and told them I'd be out there in a few minutes.

"Teri let me speak to you for a minute." Shakim's mom came over to me.

"Can this wait? I need to find my sister."

"No it can't." I blew my breath in the air and folded my arms across my chest as I waited for her to speak.

"Ever since you came in my son's life, it's been nothing but drama. He was almost killed trying to save you. In the club, my cousin was shot at over a guy who tried to talk to you and then to make matters worse, you're pregnant and I haven't heard one fucking word from you."

"Excuse me!" My attitude and anger was growing by the minute.

"You heard me. What type of woman gets pregnant by a man and doesn't include his mother when it comes to things for the baby? I haven't been to any doctor's appointment, or received a sonogram picture. So my question for you is, are you really pregnant by my son?"

"Tionne, I'm gonna act like you didn't just ask Teri no shit like that." Shakim's stepfather said.

"Yes, I did. Any woman having a man's child always tells the parents and lets them be a part of the process."

"Shawn, I'm gonna go."

"Go ahead Teri. I'll handle this." I went to walk off and felt her grabbing my arm.

"Tionne, what the hell are you doing?"

"Miss, did you just try and grab my daughter?" I heard my mom's voice and turned to see her walking in our direction.

"What is your white ass gonna do and bitch she ain't even your biological daughter. How the fuck you raising a black child anyway? It should be a law against that shit." I could see how bad it hurt my mom to hear her say that.

"Yo ma, what the fuck you just say?" Shak came storming over.

"It's ok babe." I stood in front of him.

286

"Teri, it's not ok for this woman to grab you for no reason. What if you fell and lost my grandbaby?"

"HOLD THE FUCK UP! MA, WHY THE FUCK ARE YOU EVEN TOUCHING HER?"

"Mazza can you please get him?" I was scared he'd do something he'd regret and I didn't want that. At the end of the day, she is his mother and I refused to be the reason for their bond to be broken.

"Nah, fuck that. Ma, did you put your hands on her?" His mom looked petrified as he towered over her.

"Shakim how do you know the baby is even yours? Didn't she break up with you? How do you know she didn't sleep with another man and is trying to trap you?" Shak turned to me.

"Teri, are you…" He never got to finish because I slapped fire from his ass.

"B…" He caught himself before calling me out my name.

"You told me to check on my sister and I haven't even been able to because your mother had to say something to me,

287

she claims couldn't wait until another time. But let's be clear Shak. One thing I don't play about is my family and you know this. So far, your mom has disrespected me, grabbed me so hard I almost lost my footing, basically told my mom she had no business raising me and has now said this child isn't yours. The only reason I haven't put my hands on her yet is because she's your mom. I will say she has one more time to come for me and I'm gonna forget who the fuck she is and beat her ass." He stood there looking stupid.

"You think because I'm white, you can speak to me anyway you want?" We all turned to my mom who kicked her shoes off and ran up on his mother. My mother started punching her and while I appreciated the gesture, Shak's mom response was a little much for my mom."

"Break this shit up." I heard big Faz say and pull them apart.

"Shakim, you know how your mother is, so why the fuck you even second guess anything she said. Teri, go find your sister and Ms. Bailey, I'm gonna have to teach you how to fight black women because even tho you had some good

288

punches, the windmill don't work in this day and age." She smacked him on the arm, which made me laugh.

"Teri?" I heard Shak calling my name.

"I'll call you when the baby comes. You can have a DNA test and we'll co-parent. Stay the fuck away from me nigga." I opened the door to the stairwell and my eyes grew big.

"OH MY GOD!"

To Be Continued…..

CPSIA information can be obtained
at www.ICGtesting.com
Printed in the USA
LVHW04s1544240918
591190LV00011B/1020/P